Desire at Sea

Ela Bell

ISBN-13: 978-0-9863327-7-7

DEDICATION

To my husband, my family and friends.

Acknowledgments

About the Author

Ela Bell

ACKNOWLEDGMENTS

To my husband for editing the story, to W. Stevens, to Tatiana Villa for the cover and for friends who read the book.

CHAPTER 1

Kara wondered whether her friend Sadie had found what she really wanted in Spenser. Though she felt a little lonely after Sadie had left for the UK, Kara had a good amount of self-esteem, even if it had been battered over the years. She had enough sense of personal value to think that someone cared about her besides the people she worked with at the office. She'd worked hard to get to where she was, top accountant at her firm. She'd taken not only accounting courses but also legal courses to help her understand the law. In addition, she'd studied the market. She'd invested wisely and had built a little nest for herself. She wasn't like her friends, Val and Sadie. They had money. She had had to work hard for every penny.

For Kara, life was about work, and about working to escape her past. She'd grown up in a harsh environment. Her stepfather had beat his children unmercifully. A professional boxer, he'd not pulled back on his punches or the striking. Each strike was meant to damage them. He himself had grown up receiving the same treatment, so it seemed quite natural for him to do the same to his own children.

As a child, Kara worked to figure out how to avoid the beatings. Her stepfather was quite inventive in his methods of torture. Sometimes she'd pass out and wake up with cuts and bruises. Sometimes, she'd limp to school. Eventually, she'd found a way to get around some of the beatings by working extra hard. She'd do her chores and her siblings' — polishing the wood floors with paste wax and buffing them, cleaning the bathrooms and the kitchen, dusting the furniture and making dinner — all of this between 3:30 and 6 p.m. when he arrived home. After the chores – her mother and sister sometimes cut her a break by cooking – she'd buckle down to homework. It was there that she'd shone the most.

Math was one of the pleasures she found satisfying. While she enjoyed her mother's reading and had picked up the habit herself, it was the math and eventually the accounting that led to her freedom. When she came of age, she began to lock her bedroom door. They'd given her her own room because she'd made such good grades. So he said. However, her stepfather had the habit of trying to get into her room. She found that she never slept because she felt it necessary to watch out for herself. She constantly locked the door and rose to check that it was locked. She went to school with dark circles under her eyes.

Yet, she was able to do the work a bookkeeper did and then later mastered the concepts involved in accounting. She was the lead accountant at a Manhattan firm and prided herself on noticing the details. Because of the harsh childhood she'd had, she locked people out of her heart. She was on her way out the office as she contemplated these things. She thought back to a day when her stepfather had tied up his children and beat them as though this was the only satisfaction he'd have in his day; that day, something inside her broke. She gave up hope that humans could be good or fair or decent. However, always having been a keen observer of others, she realized that revealing that side of her view of humankind would not benefit her, so she kept that side of herself carefully hidden and went about her business as though she were as capable of healthy relationships as anyone else.

The reality of her circumstance could not be hidden from her friends, however. In her last encounter with Sadie, she'd been advised to give herself permission to experience pleasure. That ability to feel anything was buried deep inside Kara. She hadn't felt the need to get in touch with her sexual feelings, so she spent time with those she cared for by giving them pleasure.

She did not, however, allow them to return the favor. She asked them to respect her need to give, not receive. But since Sadie had advised her to write down statements affirming her worthiness for not only sexual but also intimate relationships, she'd thought long and hard about her circumstances. Did she think she deserved to be loved? Did she feel the ability to allow someone to touch her, really touch her in the way that Sadie allowed a person to make love to her? Sadie was so orgasmic that she was able to come with very little provocation. Kara, partly because of her emotional anxiety about intimacy, was unable to let go.

But it wasn't long after Sadie had gone off to find her life with Spenser that Kara began to give some careful attention to Sadie's suggestions. She'd visited a therapist and talked through some of her issues, but she wasn't certain she could reach the same level of happiness and satisfaction as her friends. It was puzzling and frustrating for her since she had everything she needed in the way of economic needs — good food, adequate shelter, appropriate clothing – and some friends.

She'd distanced herself from her dysfunctional family. The thing about living in crowded circumstances, even if you are somewhat middle class, is that things can easily deteriorate into violent, vicious behavior. Most people who live in such crowded circumstances don't intend to be so base in their behavior, but human beings are animals of a sort.

Kara had witnessed her share of that, not only from her stepfather, but also from other relatives who'd moved in on the family over the years. She realized as soon as she'd passed her exams in her final semester of college that it was time to put as much distance between them and her for the sake of sanity.

She'd moved out and had been living hand to mouth on scholarships and what little work she could find while she attended school. When she graduated, she applied to firms throughout the country and was finally accepted at a small firm in New York. From there, she worked her way up the corporate ladder, ignoring any complaints her colleagues made about long hours and low pay. For her, the alternative, returning to a violent home environment where she'd be at the mercy of the same dynamics at work in her childhood, was not an option. So she worked long hours through the weekday and the weekend.

When she'd found a little fellowship with Sadie and her crowd, it was just by chance. She'd stopped by a local deli to get a bite to eat, and Sadie and her friends were crowded in a corner, quietly talking about their night out. She couldn't help staring at them, a group of women who seemed in tune with one another. Sadie winked at her, waved her over. Kara pointed at herself as if to say, "Me, you mean me?" She looked around to be certain Sadie hadn't made a mistake. Sure enough, there was no one else there. She walked over to them, and they pulled her into their world. Still, her life hadn't changed too much. She still made lists, was obsessive about everything being neat in her condo, and shared little about her emotional landscape. Somehow, Sadie seemed to guess what her trouble was and, little by little, had coaxed Kara to participate more with the group of women.

When Sadie met Spenser and had a whirlwind romance, Kara worried about her. Their friend Nita checked in on Kara every now and then. However, Kara always insisted that she was OK. And she was. Her life was tidy and organized. She had a routine that made life predictable. She worked hard during the summer months and through fall and winter. As the season for ballet and symphony performances began, she bought tickets to her favorite shows. She went alone as Sadie's friends didn't seem to relish the fine arts. Those who were left after Sadie moved to the UK were busily engaged in their own lives. So, she thought it was best to keep to herself and enjoy her little pleasures as she could find them. Those were few and far between, but certainly worth the wait.

Kara bought tickets to see "Swan Lake." She'd bought the best seat available and dressed in her finest. One of the little luxuries she allowed herself was a few nice gowns per season so that when she went to the ballet, she felt that she was going someplace special. She'd let her long brown hair hang down her back and had dressed it with sparkling pins and a bit of ribbon. Her green eyes glittered at the excitement of the other patrons. Kara's bronze skin shone with a healthy glow. She clutched a small black bag to her bosom as she entered the orchestra area to the front of the theater. She waited while other patrons stood so that she could make her way to the center of the seats.

As she walked sideways toward the center seats, a man was moving toward the center as well. Dressed in a tuxedo, he was about her height, about six feet and dressed in shiny black dress shoes and stark white dress shirt. His dark hair was combed back from his face, a little of it falling over his brow as he nodded his head to the patrons rising for his trek to his seat.

As she reached the middle seat, she noticed that a seat beside hers was also vacant; she sat down and saw that the man who was heading toward her was waiting for her to settle in her seat. He offered to help her with her wrap and in the gentlest most considerate manner, lifted it from her shoulders and placed it between the seats. He then sat down. When he sat, she smelled a fragrance emanating from him, bay and sage, mixed with something sweet, maybe honey. She sniffed without looking in his direction, but could feel him looking at her.

The conductor came out, bowed to the audience and gestured to the symphony, which had been tuning up for the performance and now sat in readiness for the show to begin. The curtain rose to a sleeping Prince Siegfried who dreams about the beautiful Odette. The evil knight Rothbart overcomes her in short order, and she turns into a swan. She's destined to be a swan by day and a maiden by night. The story unfolded before her with a cast of beautiful dancers dressed in varied shades of blue and white and an excellently played score by Tchaikovsky. As the sounds of the oboes and violins swelled and rolled in rapturous tempo to tell the story of ill-fated Odette and Siegfried, Kara felt tears roll down her cheeks. The man beside her handed her a handkerchief. She accepted it gratefully. When intermission arrived, Kara watched to see which side of the row cleared out first. The man beside her stood and offered her his hand to help her rise. She took it, rose from her chair as he placed a hand on her elbow. He guided her to the right and out to the foyer.

Overcome with the sadness and beauty of the story, she took a seat on an available bench as the man disappeared into the crowd. He returned with two flutes of champagne and offered her one. Nervous, she drank it down and he settled beside her. He took her empty flute and placed it on a small table beside them.

"My name's Alex Murdoch," he said in a pleasant bass voice. He held out a hand to her and she seemed to think about whether she wanted to engage in that custom, but then held her hand out gingerly. He caressed her hand lightly, rubbing a thumb on the back of it. He smiled at her, his brown eyes twinkling.

"Kara," she smiled. "Kara Carlisle."

"Are you enjoying the show?"

"Yes, it's sad. I've seen it before, of course, but each time, the story seems to overwhelm me."

"It is a sad tale, but it's art. The beauty of art is that it can make us think about our own lives. It helps us exorcise our demons. Whatever they may be."

His dark good looks seemed to radiate kindness.

"Do you attend the ballet often?" he asked.

"Every season, I try to catch some shows on the schedule. So I attend about three shows a season. How about you?"

"I'm a sea captain in town for a short time. I catch as many shows as I can — wherever I am at the time. That may be once a year, if I'm lucky. We happened to be in port in the New Jersey area, so I made my way here."

Kara contemplated his words as the reminder bell for the onset of the last part of the show sounded in the foyer. It wasn't quite time to return to their seats, but she liked to get there before the other patrons so that she didn't have to walk down the aisle with so many people who would then have to get out of their seats to allow her to get to her own.

"I…I like to return to my seat a little early in order not to inconvenience the others in our row."

"Oh, yes, by all means." He stood and offered her a hand up. They entered the orchestra area and found their way back to their seats. As Alex sat beside her, she took a quick moment to observe his appearance. Besides the clean lines of his tuxedo, his dark hair and dark skin gave him an overall handsome appearance that made her shiver a bit. She'd not seen such a handsome man in some time. He seemed unpretentious and unaffected by her stare. She knew that he knew that she was looking at him. Really looking. She turned away toward the stage as he turned to smile at her.

"So what do you do for a living, Kara?"

"I'm an accountant."

"So you keep track of the funds. For a large organization?"

"Yes, fairly."

"I have an idea. You can say no if you don't like it, of course. How about having dinner with me after the show?" Silence. She seemed to be fiddling with her bag.

"I. Umm. I usually don't…"

"Come on, what harm could there be in just having dinner with me? There's a nice restaurant not too far from here. We'll be in public. We can walk from here, or take a cab. No harm." He smiled at her. It was that smile — brilliant white teeth and an unpretentious attitude. He seemed friendly. As she was about to say yes, the curtains opened and the last act of the ballet began. She left the answer hanging, with a bit of tension between them.

Alex was certain she would say yes. It would be nice if she'd say it before the show ended. He wanted to take out his phone and make the reservations for them. She was one of the most attractive women he'd seen in quite a while and he'd seen his share of women around the world. His work as a merchant marine captain took him far afield. He fancied himself a connoisseur of fine women. This one exuded that sort of fineness. But, there was an underlying sadness to her that seemed to make her mysterious. She was like a puzzle that he wanted to sort out. Her long, shiny chestnut hair shone in the dim lights of the theater. Her green eyes glittered. Her face had a symmetry to it that was beautiful. She had full plump lips that looked like a man could enjoy licking and sucking. Her nose was straight and narrow. Her almond shaped green eyes seemed to suggest a knowing. He wanted to stare into them to unlock her secrets.

Her thin eyebrows framed her eyes. He found himself wanting to touch her skin, which was bronzed as though she spent her life in a tanning salon. But he knew better; this was her natural skin color. It was a beautiful dark color, reminding him of coffee. She was feminine and delicate looking. Something about her made him want to scoop her up and carry her away with him, tuck her somewhere safe and make her happy. But women rarely liked that kind of attention. He knew. He had known one who was in some ways like this woman. Not in looks, no. But, in temperament. He used one finger to trace the pleat in his trousers. The movement made her look in his direction. For a few minutes more she appeared to be focused on the show. Then she leaned over and whispered in his ear.

"Yes, I'll go to dinner with you."

Alex smiled, and pulled out his cell phone. He clicked a button and slipped it back into his tux. Later, they took a cab to the restaurant, skirting around Central Park. When they were seated, he asked her about her preference for drink, as the restaurant had a full complement of wines and champagne. After some consideration, she ordered Cuvee Sublime. "Excellent choice," he smiled, and ordered scotch for himself.

When dinner arrived – an assortment of sushi dishes — they dug into their portions and shared their appreciation of the chef's accomplishment. As he continued to pour champagne in her glass, she realized that she was having too much and refused more. But they were having such a good time that she didn't realize she'd over imbibed until she tried to stand up. He caught her at her elbow to balance her, and they left the restaurant, satisfied and happy. As they walked in the cool early spring air, Alex wondered whether he might get her to join him for a bit longer.

"Could I interest you in a little light entertainment after the show?" he asked, steering her around a group of tourists who appeared to be looking for one of the many restaurants in the area.

"I had planned on going home after the show, but…I really don't have anything special planned for tonight. What do you have in mind?"

"I have a suite at the Carlyle Hotel," he felt her stiffen a bit. "I'm not suggesting that we go to my room. The hotel has an excellent bar that features live entertainment. I thought you might want to relax a little more. I'd like to get to know you better. We're walking in that direction anyway."

"Oh," she said, stopping abruptly. "I lost track of where I was going. Umm. Yes, OK." Kara realized that she was probably letting the champagne talk for her, but Alex seemed friendly. There were plenty of people about. She could always use the opportunity to sober up a bit before catching a cab back home.

"Good, I'm happy to hear you say that. The hotel is not far from here." They walked the few blocks from 3rd avenue to 76th street and then to Bemelmans.

"Are you dating anyone?" he asked. He'd noticed that she wore no wedding band.

"I'm not. I really don't have anyone in my life right now." That was true. It was good to suggest that there might be possibilities in the future.

"I noticed that you're not wearing a wedding ring," he said.

"That would be correct. Same for you, it seems."

"The kind of business I'm in isn't good for marriage, not at least earlier in my life."

"You seem like the type of man who gets plenty of attention. You know what they say about sailors – a woman in every port?"

"I don't want to disappoint you," he chuckled. "But that's not the way most people in my business conduct their lives."

"So what does a sea captain do?" she asked, smiling up

at him.

"Mostly tell other people what to do. It can get complicated. I make certain everything is in order for the smooth running of the ship. Mostly, I allow my staff to do their jobs. I find that's the best way to run a ship – trust your crew to do their jobs. Most people want to do a good job."

"You said you were in town from another port. Does that mean you'll be leaving soon?"

"Unfortunately, yes. I'm due to take a large cargo to Europe. But after that, I'm planning on finding a place in Maine where I can live a different kind of life."

"Are you retiring?"

"In a manner of speaking, yes. I've been doing this for about 14 years now. I've made some plans to settle, do something a bit different. This business is not the kind you want to do for an extended time. Some people do, but it's getting more and more dangerous."

"What could be dangerous about transporting cargo?"

"Pirates."

"Oh, I've heard about those. They're mostly off the coast of Somalia, right?"

"Yes, mostly there, but you can find them off the coast of Nigeria and in parts of the Indian Ocean."

"Can't merchant marine ships defend themselves from pirates?"

"That's a good question. Some mariners and the politicians in their countries of origin believe carrying weapons will do nothing but encourage pirates to escalate their attacks. But, many of us do arm ourselves in some way."

"Seems like a good idea," she said. They'd arrived at the hotel. Alex held the door for Kara, and they walked into the bar. Images of children playing in a park, people sitting on benches, balloons being sold to patrons were part of the wallpaper in the bar. Kara felt a swell of playful delight at

11

the paintings of people having a pleasant day.

The band played mellow jazz; it was not too loud for patrons to have a conversation. Patrons dressed well at this lounge. They were shown to a table that had leather backed brown sofas on one side and chairs on the other. She was surprised that Alex sat down beside her on the leather sofa instead of across from her on one of the wooden chairs. When the waiter arrived, they ordered drinks – Kara asking for a non-alcoholic drink. They sat together listening to the music. After a bit, he gestured to her as a request to dance. They rose and joined the other participants. As Alex led her onto the dance floor, she noticed his smooth confident movement. He held her close as they danced slowly. When the music stopped, they returned to their table and listened to the set until the band took a break. When Kara yawned into her hand, Alex realized he had kept her up beyond her bedtime. His cell phone buzzed with a text message. He took it out, read it and placed it back into his jacket.

"Would you like me to see you home or would you care to join me for a night cap in my suite?" he asked.

"I think I'd better plan to go home," she said. "It's late; though I don't go to work tomorrow, I normally don't stay out this late. I guess you can tell."

He smiled. "You're welcome to stay at my suite if you want. I promise I don't bite. There are two beds; I promise to get you back home first thing tomorrow." Kara contemplated what he said.

"As much as I appreciate the offer, I think I'd better be returning home. I normally don't spend this much time out with…"

"With men?"

"Actually, not with anybody."

"That can't be good for you."

"Actually, it's fine for me. I prefer it that way." He tilted his head and looked at her as though trying to solve a puzzle. He smiled, the corner of one side of his mouth pulling down.

"At least let me see you home then. I couldn't live with myself otherwise."

She seemed to consider this for a moment. "Just so you know that it doesn't mean an invitation to spend the night at my place."

"Point taken," he grinned. "Now, let's get you home." He called the waiter over and asked him to summon a cab. Since cabs frequented the area, there was little problem getting one. A short ride to her condo and a walk to her door and he was helping her to get the door open.

"May I see you tomorrow?"

"I thought you wouldn't be in town much longer."

"Actually, I'll be here a day or so as the ship is repaired and loaded with some additional containers. Then I'm off to Europe, probably Amsterdam – a short trip. Since I won't have too many days in port this time, I thought perhaps we could hang out some." She seemed to ponder this a bit before answering.

"Relax," he whispered, reaching for her hand. He held it to his lips to kiss it. She blushed realizing that she'd never had someone kiss her hand. What an unusual man. He grinned at her. In that moment, she could see some element of innocence in him, but also a little mischievousness.

"There's a little cafe around the corner from here," she said. "Give me your cell number, and I'll text you a link for it." They exchanged numbers and agreed to meet for brunch.

CHAPTER TWO

When Alex awoke the next morning, his cell phone rang. His first officer, Maximina Savoy, was calling to update him on the ship's readiness for its voyage to the Netherlands and the projected weather patterns for the northern Atlantic. He'd showered and shaved and had dressed in a pair of jeans and a blue shirt for his brunch with Kara. Max was as capable as they came, so he never worried about the details of the ship's readiness.

"Hey, Max," he answered.

"Captain, just wanted to let you know that we might be delayed another day or two. The repairs are on schedule, but it seems one of the companies wants us to hold for some additional containers to arrive. Also, there might be another trip chartered for us after this one, perhaps a stop in South Africa."

Silence. After a moment, Alex realized he was giving her the impression that he wasn't on the phone.

"Captain?"

"Yeah, Max, I'm here. I'm just disappointed. My impression was that it would be the one run to the

Netherlands."

"I know, sir, but they emailed a bill of lading for additional goods. They say that they emailed you about it. I just wanted to check before I proceeded further."

"Give me a minute, Max." Alex walked to his laptop and checked his email. The email suggested the last minute goods needed to be delivered in Singapore. They might have to return for that shipment after the trip to Rotterdam in the Netherlands. That meant a longer voyage than they'd originally planned. The long voyage to Singapore would begin after a return to the states. They would put to sea from New Jersey, stop briefly in South Africa and continue to Singapore.

"Thanks, Max, for the heads up. I'll get in touch with them. Go ahead and allow the loading up to our maximum. I'll be there tomorrow to check on the load and crew."

"See you then, Captain." Alex put the phone down and looked at the email again. This shipment could be dry goods or it could be an assortment of medical supplies and computer equipment. Whatever the containers included, the risk of encountering a storm or attack by pirates was a real concern, as he'd been discussing with Kara the previous night. They had delayed for a bit for repairs and to avoid a predicted late spring storm; it would be necessary to get on with the transit as soon as the danger had passed.

A course would need to be set for the additional voyage with plans for avoiding pirates. He wrote to the managers involved explaining the risks, which they were certainly aware of but needed to be reminded of, and asked that additional costs be added. After addressing other details and email from his welder and second officer, he shut down his computer and headed out to meet Kara. While on his way to meet her, he made a special reservation, hoping she'd like it.

***

Kara sat at a table on the small patio outside the restaurant. Braziers heated the patio as patrons enjoyed mimosas and various breakfast dishes. Alex spotted her by the smile she wore. A light red jacket and matching red maxi dress graced her curves as she stood up to greet him. She was taller than average, he noticed. He bussed her on both cheeks in the manner of the French and Italians and sat down.

"Good morning," he said. "You're looking pretty, rested and happy. I hope I have something to do with that."

"I won't lie. I had a good night's rest and looked forward to seeing you," she said. She didn't add that she'd lain awake for about two hours thinking of him and wondering whether their budding friendship would turn into a dead end for her as so many other relationships had. But she was pulled from her thoughts by the arrival of the waitress. They gave her their menus. A few minutes later, she arrived with a mimosa for Kara and coffee for Alex.

"Do you come here often?" Alex noticed that she tended to daydream a bit. There was sometimes a lag in her response to his questions.

"When I want to get out and away from things, yes. It's a pleasant little café. Some of them are disappearing, so I think it's important to get out and enjoy them while we can."

"Sounds like a good plan." He took a sip of his coffee and placed the mug on the table. "Good coffee."

"I noticed you take it black; is that because you need to be ready to respond on your ship?" He chuckled.

"No, that's because I like it black and have since I was quite young. I noticed you don't seem to like coffee."

"No, I prefer tea, mostly herbal teas. I prefer Chamomile and Rooibos teas, the sort that calms." Alex made a mental note to probe a little more to find out why "calming" was necessary if she lived alone. It must be something in her past.

"I found out this morning that my departure will be delayed a bit. The next leg of my duties will bring me back here but for an extended trip."

Kara felt some measure of disappointment. Why am I feeling this way? I don't know him well enough to give a damn whether he returns next week or next year. What am I thinking? She didn't know what to say.

"Um. You said you'll be here for a little more time. Are you going to be in this area?" Dumb question. It was just something to say. She couldn't think of anything else.

"I need to go to New Jersey for part of a day, but that's not far. After that, I'll have some time to visit." He let some time pass as they ate their meal.

"Mmm. They do a good job on their quiche," he said. It was a good thing to say to break the tension. He didn't want to pressure her to spend time with him. After all, they'd just met, but there was something about Kara, besides her beauty and sumptuous figure, that made him want to be with her. He had been thinking for a while about changing things in his life. Working at sea could be rewarding, but also risky. Lately, he'd felt something was missing from his life and wondered whether someone like Kara might be the answer.

"My favorite breakfast food is this vegetarian omelet," she said. She held the cloth napkin to her mouth and dabbed daintily.

"Would you like to spend the day with me, Kara? We could do a little sightseeing, some shopping — on me, of course — or just hang out doing this or that."

"I'd like that," she said, before she realized she'd said it. She was surprised to hear him say the word "shopping" as most men didn't like doing that sort of thing. She admitted to her friends that she didn't quite care too much for shopping as online purchases saved time, but with someone else offering to foot the bill and even keep her company, it sounded fun.

She thought about the time she would spend away from her work and considered whether she wanted to invest time in a relationship with someone who spent most of his life at sea. However, he did say he was at the end of that life, and anyway, this was just a trial. They might not ever see each other after these few days. Or, it might be just the thing for her. He wouldn't get in the way of her personal life if he didn't work or live in the area. Not that she had much of one; she did enjoy her own company.

"What do you have in mind first?" she asked.

"I thought we'd go on a tour of the harbor. There's an interesting clipper ship that you might like. Then, maybe just see where our fancy takes us. What do you say?"

"I like that idea. I don't think I've ever thought to board a ship. I've been on the ferry of course, but that's different. It might be interesting."

They made their way to Battery Park where the ship was waiting for passengers to board. He'd made a reservation for them, so when they boarded, he gave their names. They settled in with other passengers as the tour began; Kara grinned like a schoolgirl as the ship lingered near the Statue of Liberty and then slowly made its way toward other parts of the tour, which included an opportunity to hoist the sails and ask questions of the crew. Alex guided Kara to the bow and helped her find a place to watch the sights.

"I suppose you get to do this all the time," she said looking up at him. He put an arm around her shoulders as the breeze made the early spring weather a bit chilly. She shivered in his embrace.

"Not really. When you're part of a crew on a ship, you really don't think much about the anatomy of it. It's business, and your mind is on it. Ships have always been a passion for me, though. This one was originally an 1854 schooner from Manitowoc, Wisconsin. She had the reputation of being one of the fastest ships of her time. She was originally built to haul heavy cargo like lumber. Since she's been rebuilt, she now has a steel hull and carries six fore and aft rigged sails and two square topsails on two steel masts." Kara let some time pass without commenting on this. It seemed natural that he'd be informed about something he did for a living. "This kind of ship was part of my early collection of miniatures."

"Really, how many did you collect?"

"As a child and a teenager, probably hundreds. I lost count."

"Sounds like an expensive hobby."

"It was, but there was only me and my sister in our family. We didn't lack for much. It was part of my father's interest too. So I made it my own. Each time he went to sea, I knew what kind of ship he sailed on and traced the navigational route. When he returned home, we'd spend hours talking about his adventures, the places he went."

"Sounds like you had a good relationship with your father." Alex looked at Kara. She stiffened, seeming to tense at that comment. It seemed odd since she'd made the observation.

"We did. Like any father and son, we had our challenging moments. He didn't want me to sail, wanted me to stay on land. It became a source of contention between us when he retired."

"So are both your parents…."

"They're both living. I don't see them often, but when I do, we enjoy time together. What about your parents?" She took a deep breath and stepped away from him, pretending to find interest in something in the distance.

"My stepfather and mother are living, but I don't see them. We're…I ah. I mean. We have a difficult relationship. I try not to see them often."

"I'm sorry to hear that, Kara." He allowed the sounds of the sails billowing in the wind and the sound of the rigging clocking against the ship to fill their ears. Other passengers talked quietly. He could feel her tense as he reached for her and placed his arm around her again. He kissed her on the cheek and said nothing. They walked to the portside of the ship as a beer-tasting event began.

***

When Alex took a cab to Kara's condo, they'd had dinner and wine and were exhausted from a long day in the wind. He unlocked the door for her and opened it.

"Would you like to come in?" she asked. He nodded and stepped forward.

She hung their coats in a hall closet and led the way to her living room. Her place was decorated in warm reds and browns, with antique furniture placed at intervals that suggested an interior decorator had taken time to place every piece at a perfect angle. She had fresh flowers on one large table in the foyer and a grandfather clock at the right of the living room. The clock went off as they walked in, causing Alex to turn to it. Other clocks went off as well. A cuckoo clock on the wall, a Howard Miller mantel clock and a variety of other clocks began the half hour clanging as they entered the room. She gestured to the couch and went to the kitchen to get wine.

"I can see that you're passionate about clocks," he said, deciding not to sit right away but instead walking to the grandfather clock to give it a look. It had modern lines to it, but a traditional face and pendulum. "Do you have just the one grandfather clock?"

"Yes, I keep the one because it only needs winding every week. I don't relish winding clocks, so I have some that are electric, some battery operated and one wind up, the grandfather clock," she said, handing him the glass of wine. She placed snacks of nuts and fruit on the coffee table in front of them.

"You live here alone then? I would assume so since it's

so quiet."

"I tried a roommate years ago, but it was too much trouble," she sat back on the couch, flicked off her shoes and tucked her feet up under her. "My work requires that I take some of it home with me, so I really prefer a quiet home environment." He leaned back on the couch as well, his head tipping back. Before he knew it, he was dozing off. The sound of the clocks woke him much later. When he opened his eyes, Kara had fallen asleep on the sofa as well. He stood, stretched and walked a short distance to where he thought her bedroom was. Indeed, her bedroom was where he expected it, with a large sleigh bed and a collection of similar antiques. He turned down the covers and returned to her, bent his knees and scooped her up in his arms. He expected her to wake, but she didn't. He planted a light kiss on her forehead and carried her to the bedroom.

When he laid her down, he pulled the covers up to her waist and unfastened the button near her neck. He then lifted the covers up to her shoulders and walked to the other side of the bed. He took off his own shoes and lay on top of the comforter, pulled a throw over himself from the bottom of the bed and fell fast asleep.

Early that morning, at about 5 a.m., he woke to the sound of whispering wind and the sound of chimes. He was a little disconcerted at first, then realized that he was at Kara's home. He looked to his right to see Kara staring at him.

"Hello," he said quietly.

"I usually don't allow men in my bed," she said, with a tight smile. "How did I get here?"

"I carried you." She looked under the cover.

"I must have been exhausted. I usually don't sleep in my clothes either."

He reached one hand out and smoothed her hair out of her eyes. He moved closer to her. He noticed she tensed as he neared.

"Kara, may I ask you a question?"

"Sure," she said, looking up to the ceiling.

"You seem to be uncomfortable around me. Is it me or just all men?"

"It's not you." He could hear the ticking of her clocks in the other rooms of her home.

"Do you prefer women? I mean some women do. I thought it might be…"

"As a matter of fact, I prefer the company of some women. The kind who are quiet and kind." She didn't want to explain that there had been one fated attempt by one man to gain her interest, but that had not worked.

"You do?" Alex took a deep breath and turned on his back. "I guess then that there's no hope for us. I am kind. But sometimes I can get loud. And as you can see…." He grinned. "I'm not a woman."

"I, um, I have a hard time. I actually have a friend, a girlfriend, who."

"You and she are involved?"

"No, I told you earlier. She recently married." Silence.

"Were you in love with her?"

"I don't think I know what that means." Alex pulled a face. Then, he turned toward her again.

"Would you mind if I kiss you?" She didn't answer, so Alex drew nearer and put one hand lightly on her face. He used one finger to brush her face lightly. Her skin was soft and delicate. With his thumb, he gently smoothed over her bottom lip, then he kissed her lips lightly. He pulled back and looked at her. Her eyes were wide as she looked at him.

"How was that?"

"I liked it."

"Would you let me do it again? I mean, kiss you." He pressed his lips against hers again and this time used his tongue to lick her lips and tease them open. The kissing began to intensify as he turned his head this way and that to suck and lick at her lips and then to his surprise, she darted her tongue out just briefly to lick at his lips. He pulled back and looked at her, his breathing heavy.

"Could we try that again?" he asked. They did. This time, Alex placed a hand on her shoulder and ran it down her arm to her fingertips. He played with each finger, pulling each one gently as he licked and sucked gently at her lips. Kara could feel herself losing control and struggled desperately to bring herself back into line, but for some reason, she couldn't seem to think clearly.

She felt Alex place a hand on her breast and move it inside her blouse. She pulled back from him then, breathing heavily as well. He didn't move his hand but continued to massage her breast; she could feel his hand cupping it lightly and then running his rough-worn thumb over her nipple.

"Kara, I promise only to go as far as you want." She nodded her head and closed her eyes. Just then, she felt him shift his weight to undo the buttons on her blouse and then the button that held her jeans closed. When he did this, she grabbed his hand and held it tight. He stopped.

"Alex, I don't think I can do this."

"Why, sweetheart? Tell me why you can't do it. I'm not asking to penetrate you. I just want to give you a little pleasure." *Liar.* He wanted more than that, at least that's what his burgeoning cock said; it was about to pop out of his jeans. But he sensed that she was someone who would not allow a man to take her too fast. He kissed her again, this time deeply and with a hunger she felt to her center. He pressed a hand on her belly and teased her there then moved slowly under her clothes and to her thatch of curls. He played in her pubic hair for a while, moving his fingers slowly toward the nub where her sex had begun to get moist. She heard a low moan, seconds later, surprised that it had come from her. With one finger, he played with the tip of her clitoris, rubbing it back and forth. Every now and then he played on the side, rubbing the wet, moist fluid around her sex. All the while, he continued to kiss her, licking and sucking gently on her lips as though this was what he planned to do between her thighs. She thrust her hips to meet the movement of his finger. He pulled back from her and looked into her eyes, one hand still at work on her button.

"Kara, sweetheart," he nearly whispered. He kissed her again, this time with one hand on her face. He kissed her eyelids and nose, each cheek before he returned to her lips. "Sweet, you're so sweet. Will you trust me, sweetheart? Can you let go for me? Come for me. Can you do that?" She moaned. The sound of her voice nearly made him explode. He tried to think of ship business in order to focus on her pleasure.

Kara tried to hold back the feelings that were swirling about in her. Her breasts tingled and the space between her legs felt like warm wet jelly. She could feel something building, an urgency, a need. Something in her belly tightened and then her hips as she reached for it. Her mind disengaged, and she began to feel light and feathery as her passage contracted and released again and again. She could hear herself cry out as the orgasm took control, spinning her into a state of near unconsciousness.

She closed her eyes and floated, the feeling of warmth and jubilation sweeping over her so that she lost her place in the landscape of her emotions and her world. When she floated back to earth, she opened her eyes and saw him looking at her with the tenderest expression that her breath caught in her throat. A tear formed at the corner of her eye.

"Are you OK?" he asked smiling. She grinned.

"I…I never…Um I've never felt anything like that. It was…"

"The French call it le petit mort, the little death, because it disengages you from everything." He brushed her hair from her face and kissed her lightly.

"What about you?" she asked. "Can you show me what you need?"

He looked down at his erect penis, straining to get out of his pants. She reached for it and smoothed her hand over it. He flinched. She zipped down his fly and smiled at him. "Let me help you," he said, his voice hoarse with need.

"It wouldn't take much." His rod sprung from his pants, engorged and glistening at the tip. He placed his hand on top of hers and guided her in the movement. She rubbed a thumb over the tip of his cock and then her soft hand circled it barely fitting around his girth. She began to move her hand up and down his long cock, using the other to cup his balls. He moved his hand over hers and thrust once, twice and came, a jet stream of milky fluid spurting on his belly. He murmured some throaty exclamations of satisfaction, then, breathing heavily, lay back to regroup. She handed him a hand towel from the bedside table to clean himself, and then she moved close to him, and he encircled her in his arms.

When they woke, the later morning hour announced its presence with the sound of birds, traffic and people outside. Her apartment was in a high-rise, but the muted sounds of life reached them from the street. He reached for her, but there was no Kara. Then he smelled the aroma of rich coffee and knew he'd landed. This woman knew coffee. She walked into the room dressed in a robe and with her hair wrapped in a towel.

"You're up early for having had a late night," he stood and stretched. She handed him a cup of coffee. He took a sip.

"Ah, that hit the spot. However," he held up one finger. "I do like to freshen up a bit before having my coffee. Could I trouble you for an extra…"

"There are extra toothbrushes and plenty of towels in the linen closet. I'll be getting dressed while you shower."

"You must have lots of company to be so prepared," he

said from the bathroom. "Any chance you have a razor? I'd like to shave."

"Don't push your luck." She chuckled. "I have visitors from time to time, though none lately. You might find a pink razor somewhere in there, but I can't vouch for how sharp it is." She walked to her closet and took out some jeans and walked to her dresser to get underclothes. She changed the sheets and covers on the bed and stored them in a hamper and then walked to a dresser drawer to get underclothes. She had just put her bra on and was slipping a pair of white bikini underwear on when Alex walked into the room. Her back was to him. He froze as he starred at the scars on her back and legs. She turned her head around to see him staring at her and began to tremble. He rushed to her and enveloped her in his arms.

He turned her around by the shoulders and kissed her tenderly and hugged her. He bent down a bit to look into her eyes. "Kara," he whispered. Tears began to fall. She wiped them away. "Don't," she said. "Don't! Don't!" She tried to push him away.

"Don't what, sweetheart?"

"Don't look at me like that. Like I'm …Like I'm damaged, used goods, someone's throwaway." He was stunned speechless for a moment, unsure what to say.

"Kara!" he shouted so loud that she jumped. She began to shake. He put his arms around her again. "I'm sorry I startled you, honey. I just want to kill the bastard that did this to you. And the notion of your being damaged did not enter my head at all."

She pulled away and reached for her jeans, slid them on and walked to the closet to get a shirt. She put it on with her back still toward him. "Thank you for that then." Silence. She grabbed a brush and began brushing her hair.

He walked to her and held her hand as she tried to brush. "Kara, please don't shut me out. I know it may be difficult for you to trust anyone ever. But life is about finding someone you *can* trust. If your inclination is never to allow anyone to enter your life — I mean in the way of a meaningful relationship — I can understand that now." He put his hands on her shoulders and turned her around gently to face him. "Sweetheart, you have to tell me what happened and decide whether you're going to let me in your life. I'm not the kind of man who does things in half measures. When I decide to be with someone, to make a commitment, it's all the way."

"Aren't we going a little fast, Alex?" she asked. "We've only known each other a few days and you're going out to sea, maybe for months." Actually, saying the words made her feel a little better since it meant that she wasn't going to have to trust him because he wouldn't be there.

He led her to the dining area where they sat down facing one another. "I'm asking you to allow this to grow – to see what can happen. The first step is leveling with one another about things that keep us from enjoying the best of life. Now, there's no risk for you in telling me what happened to you. Who would I tell? We are going to see each other again if that's what you want. But, you need to decide whether that's going to happen." She fiddled with the cutlery on the dining table and turned her face away from him as though looking at something outside the window.

"As I said, I don't do things in half measures, and if we're going to continue to see one another," he paused. "I'd like to know who I'm going to kill." She chuckled and looked down at her feet. With one finger, he lifted her chin and kissed her lightly on the lips.

"You can't. It was my stepfather." He exhaled, stood up, paced to the window and walked back toward her. "What kind of sick bastard?"

"It was supposed to be discipline."

"Discipline is one thing, but this is. This is barbaric. How old were you?"

She took a deep breath. "It began when I was about 9

and continued through our teens."

"You have siblings?"

"Yes, can we not talk about this anymore, Alex? It's really more than I intended on sharing. I really just want to get out today. Do you mind?" He waited a few seconds before responding. He knew that this would be difficult for Kara; however, getting her to talk about it would be another thing entirely. It might be best to allow her to tell the story in pieces.

"Sounds perfect." He walked over to her and kneeled in front of her, one knee on the floor. He took her hand in his and kissed it. "There's no need to rush it. But I want you to know, Kara, that I would never treat you or anyone I care for in that manner. You can trust me to protect you and to never, ever do anything, knowingly, to hurt you."

"Knowingly?" she asked, pulling a face. She smiled. He smiled.

"I think you know what I mean. Sometimes people say things to each other that they don't realize could hurt the other person. I try to be careful with my words as well. However, sometimes…" He shrugged.

"No need to explain. I didn't fall off the turnip truck. I have had some, well, kind of friendships. I think I understand what you mean. Now, shall we change the subject? That was a long time ago, and I've tried very hard to put it behind me."

"I have an idea for what we might do today if you don't mind." She tilted her head as though interested. Just then her clocks went off again in a symphony of delightful sound. He stood and brought her up by the elbows to look at him. "I have to make a quick trip to New Jersey; then, I'd like to take you out. Would you like to go shopping?"

"Alex, that's a dangerous thing to ask a woman." She grinned.

"Look, I'm only in town for a day or so more and then it's out to sea for a month or more. I don't want to waste time hording money. I want to spend it on you."

"In that case, Mr. Murdoch, I"ll be waiting when you return." Kara smiled, excited to be included in a new adventure with Alex. She wasted no time calling the office to say she would not be coming in for a few days.

Alex freshened up, returned to the hotel and changed, packed a light bag with some clothing and used a favorite car service for the trip to the Newark Elizabeth Marine Terminal. When he arrived at the docks, cranes were loading containers onto the ship. He boarded the ship, checked the bill of lading and spoke to his first officer. After a quick meeting with his officers and core crew, he gave them instructions on preparations for the first leg of their trip and checked other aspects of the voyage. The ship's mechanic was busy working on the repair to a pump, so they were forced to delay. In addition, a storm in the Atlantic would stall their departure, but a slight delay was better than risking loss of the containers. He left the dock in plenty of time to meet Kara at her place and take her shopping. They gathered their coats and belongings and headed for Times Square first and a few other choice shops.

CHAPTER THREE

Kara had never been shopping with a man. Heck, she shopped little for herself and when she did, it was usually online or for something specific. The notion of going on a shopping excursion was so unusual that she wondered if she had missed something all these years. She'd been shopping with a friend years ago, but it was hardly fun. They were really out to talk, so the shopping was an ancillary activity. This time, however, shopping was fun, not only because someone else was spending the money, but also because he seemed to enjoy it.

What was that she'd heard about men and shopping? Was it that they hated it? As they entered the first shop off Times Square, she was impressed with fragrances. But she was more impressed with his genuine interest in something she seemed to like. The clerk helped her sample a variety of scents while Alex stood close by offering his opinion of first this scent and then another, offered as samples on paper and then, if she liked it, a spritz on her wrist or the back of her hand. She finally picked out a light apple-like fragrance; he asked that the fragrance be bundled with the matching lotion, body wash and soap. When she left the shop, she felt special.

They jumped in a cab and headed to an area that had boutique shops. There, he offered his opinion as he waited patiently while she tried on this dress or that pair of jeans or a suit of some sort. They visited about three shops in all, the sales people seemingly alert as she walked in and they sized up the nature of the customer.

It seemed that when a woman entered a store with a man who appeared to be ready to spend money on her, the clerks paid close attention to her needs. It was really quite a different experience. She was accustomed to going into a store and picking out pieces without assistance. Each time she entered these shops, the clerks seemed to bring her clothes for consideration. At one store, there was someone there to model the clothes for her and Alex. From those, she picked out what she liked and Alex picked a couple he liked. This truly was different.

The coup de gras was a visit to a hair stylist and nail shop where Alex indulged himself in a pedicure to keep her company. Now, that was going to be something to tell her friends. Following that, they went to dinner and took a cab back to her place. When they returned to her apartment, she was shopped out, tired and truly impressed.

"I've never, ever done some of those things with my friends," she said, flopping down on the couch in her living room. The clocks had just finished chiming when they walked in the door.

"A man who is comfortable with his masculinity can be comfortable with a little shopping and a little pampering thrown in for extra measure. Did you enjoy yourself?"

"Claro que si, of course," she said grinning and slipping off her shoes. "I'm full and happy and haven't ever felt this pampered and spoiled. Have you done this with other armours?"

"Actually, no, I haven't. When my sister was in the mood, I'd go with her to keep her company." He became pensive.

"Was she a big shopper?"

"She would put you to shame in a New York minute," he said. "My sister, Adelaide, is the epitome of the shopaholic. If she's blue and needs a pickup, shopping is the key."

"Really, does she get blue often?" He looked to the kitchen trying to decide how much to tell her.

"Would you like some wine or something else to drink?" he asked. "I'm offering to get it for you. I bet your feet hurt."

"You're right, they do. There's wine and water in the fridge. If you'd prefer something stronger, there's a cart in the dining room." He walked to the kitchen and took two glasses from the shelf and then grabbed a bottle of wine. He poured himself a brandy from the cart and returned with the wine and a glass of water.

He drank a bit of the brandy and sat back sighing. He rarely opened up to others about his family, but she had shared some of herself with him. Since there might not be time for them to do much more together after the next day, it would be best for him to trust her with his feelings as well.

"My sister suffers from depression and has since we were young. She's fine when she stays on her medication, but when she's not taking it, she has a devil of a time." He took another sip of the brandy.

"I can understand that. I haven't suffered from it myself, but I have a relative who does." The clocks were ticking as they sat there drinking. She walked to an antique hutch that contained a stereo. She pressed a button and soft Brazilian jazz began to play. He expected that this would be something she might enjoy listening to considering her personality.

"You say you haven't suffered from it. That seems unusual. Someone who has experienced the…" He stopped realizing that he might be treading on tender territory.

"Maybe different people deal with stuff in different ways. I know what you're about to say. I should be desperately upset, but mostly I've managed my life by making the decision to distance myself from circumstances that might keep me unbalanced. So, after I left home at about 17, I didn't look back. I generally feel fine. I have seen a couple of therapists."

"Smart lady," he said. "I know you said your feet hurt, but care to take a little spin to the music?" He stood and offered her a hand. She walked into his arms and felt the sway of his hips, his hard thighs and his firm chest as he moved her around the carpeted floors with ease. They moved very little but rocked to the gentle sounds of the jazz. Finally, she yawned, and he didn't hesitate to pick her up and carry her to her room. There, he placed her gently on the bed and helped her out of her jeans and shirt. He looked at her with a question on his face as he placed a hand on his shirt to unbutton it. She nodded and smiled to him. They showered together. He took his time gently drying her off, patting here and there. When they were finished, they snuggled under the covers.

He held out his arms to her as she wiggled into his arms. Though she could feel the evidence of his arousal, she wasn't certain what he wanted. Even more, she felt nervous. There was something she should have told him. She reached her hand to his chest and smoothed down to his flat belly and then his penis. He flinched a bit when she placed her hand around his cock.

She kissed his chest and pressed her breasts into him. He placed a hand on her hair, her face, kissing her tenderly. Then, slid a hand down to her breast, kneading it gently. Slowly, he moved a hand down to her stomach and then her mons. She was wet and warm. "Kara, angel, I don't think I can wait much longer. At this rate, I'm going to lose it. Let me do this for you first." He pulled the covers down and began to kiss her small, firm breasts, sucking on one nipple and then the other. Kara could feel an answering call in her womb as he licked and sucked at her buds. He moved back up to her face and kissed her lips again, sucking gently at her bottom lip and then plunging his tongue deep into her mouth. She felt herself melting, a slippery wetness forming between her thighs. He placed his hand on her crevice and pushed down, finding her button. He moved quickly down her torso, kissing her as he went down, down and found that nest, that tender little nut covered with skin; he pulled it into his mouth and sucked it gently at first and then forcefully. Then, he licked it firmly, backing up. He fingered her folds and then her clitoris. She jumped and he pulled back, frowning.

"Come for me, angel," he said in a throaty deep masculine voice that reverberated through her. She felt a rise urgent, delicious call of his urging as he returned to her button and continued his gentle probing. Suddenly, she felt it rise in her, an orgasm so strong that she froze, stunned by the enormity of it, the voice she heard hardly sounding like her own. She could feel the contractions in her channel as she reached that peak of pleasure, spiraling up, up, up and then floating down into bliss. He withdrew his index finger and tasted her sweet juices. His cock was nearly bursting. He rose on his forearms and used one leg to spread her thighs. He positioned himself at her entrance. He pushed but felt hindered. She was so tight, so juicy.

"Sweetheart, open for me," he said. He pushed a little more inside her and felt a barrier. He frowned.

"I'm...I Alex, I forgot to tell you. I've... This is my first time with a man." He froze. No wonder. He wanted to plunge into her depths but this wasn't the time to do it. He felt something inside his chest expand as he realized he would be her first. A woman's first time with a man determined whether she would ever want to have sex again. He began to count backwards in his head to get control of himself. Finally, he kissed her briefly and looked into her eyes.

"Do you want to stop?"

"No, I think we've come too far to turn back now. I just wanted you to know. I …um, I don't know. I'm not sure what to do here."

He held himself at her entrance waiting. He leaned more on his forearms to prevent further penetration.

"We'll take it slow, OK?"

She nodded. He pushed a little more and then pulled back. Pushed in and pulled back, at each gentle push, he allowed her to grow accustomed to his cock.

"There's a rhythm to it, Kara. The key is to relax. Women say it hurts the first time, but it doesn't have to. Not much that is. So I've heard. Try to breathe and relax." He saw her trying to focus on breathing.

"Kara, I'm going to push in deeper this time. I want you to hold my shoulders. If it hurts too much tell me and I'll stop." He pushed in more and could feel something inside her throb and unravel. He looked at her for signs of distress; her head was turned away from him.

He turned her head toward his and kissed her again, this time, turning his attention to one of her breasts. He rubbed his thumb over her nipple and pressed it between his thumb and forefinger. She moaned, a long sweet, warble, deep in the back of her throat. He couldn't hold back. He pressed his full length inside her and moved in and out, short sweet strokes. He felt her hips wiggle as he found purchase in her depths.

Kara felt a slight pinch as Alex moved further inside her; something seemed to be coming to her as he stroked her deep inside. It was as though he had found a spot that tickled and had scratched that itch. She couldn't hold back. Suddenly, she felt herself coming again, her orgasms as strong as the first time. Her head moved from side to side as she gasped and then shouted. She held onto to him, squeezing his shoulders and pressing her fingers into his back.

"Alex! Alex!" His hips quickened as he stroked her once, twice and then on the third stroke, he came, crying out her name and murmuring sweet words of love to her. "Kara, darling. Sweet angel. My love. Oh sweet Cherie."

He collapsed on top her, spent and exhausted as he felt her hips cradle him. He rolled off her to keep from crushing her. They fell asleep in one another's arms and woke much later to the sound of rain on windows outside.

"Hello, sweetheart," he said as he noticed she was awake and watching him. "Are you alright?" She nodded.

"I didn't know."

"What?"

"I didn't know it could be like that," she said.

"I hope I didn't hurt you," he said, brushing her hair from her face.

"It wasn't bad at all. Just the slightest pinch. Like this." She pinched the skin on his arm. He kissed her.

"You know," he said sighing. "I could get very accustomed to this." She said nothing, but caressed his arm.

He rose and walked to the bathroom to run a bath for her. He rooted around in her toiletries cabinet to find fragrant bath salts, which he sprinkled liberally into the water. He then returned to the bed and gathered her in his arms. He walked to the bathroom and placed her before the tub. "See if the water temperature is right for you." She felt it. When she nodded, he picked her up again and stepped into the tub, lowering them both down into the fragrant water.

***

The hours that they spent together before Alex's departure were full of similar intimate moments. They took long walks, went to the Central Park Zoo, the Aquarium and to a few restaurants. On one occasion, they stayed at her place to cook for one another and enjoyed preparing different dishes. Alex had a flare for Asian dishes as he'd done quite a bit of traveling in that area. When it came time for him to leave, they confirmed their email addresses and phone numbers.

"Alex, this has been some of the best time I've spent with anyone," Kara said as he held her in his arms. "Do you think you'll be back soon?"

"I'll probably return in about six weeks if not sooner," he said tipping her chin up and giving her a soulful kiss. "Hmmm. If we continue down this road, I might not make it to my ship on time."

"I'm ordering you to depart, captain," she said, holding one hand up to her forehead in a mock salute. Kara had enjoyed their time together, but she was looking forward to the time to herself again. Sharing her life with someone else was pleasant, but she needed time to think about the way things were going.

"Aye, aye, m'am," he said, kissing her again. "We'll keep in touch, Kara. I'll email you as often as I can. It won't be long before I return. I'll be back before you know it."

She sighed and put her arms around his neck and kissed him back. "I've really enjoyed myself, Alex. Stay well," she said softly.

***

Getting out of the Elizabeth channel could get complicated if everything was not in order. They had been scheduled to depart much earlier, but there was a problem with a different cargo ship. Alex had received reports from his officers and bosun's mate to affirm a check of all matters related to departure, including confirmation that all crew were on board, stores and bunkers were replenished as well as fresh water.

At work on the navigation deck, Alex went down the list of other considerations. All crew had necessary legal documents, movable objects were checked and double-checked for possibility of movement. Generally, Alex believed in allowing his officers and other staff to do their jobs. They all knew their roles and had been at work before he'd arrived. It was rare that Alex was away from the ship for very long, so contact by email and phone was enough to assure him that the ship was in order for the voyage. Still, he checked the departure items again and checked with each of his officers before preparation to receive the harbor pilot, Jason. As a final requirement of departure, he had the reverse gear on the engine checked.

Jason had guided many ships out of the channel. He'd played along this channel as a boy and knew the channel like the back of his hand. About 40, with a bulky build and short height, he was a cheerful sort, speaking to the navigation crew in a New Jersey accent.

"Yous got to know how to make your way out of this harbah," he said chewing something vigorously, probably gum. One of the crew offered him a cup of coffee, but he waved it away. "This channel ain't like a lot of places. It's got some special traps, sand bars and things." This was no secret to Alex, but he smiled at the man, letting him do his job without interference. That was the job of the harbor pilot, to get a large cargo ship out of the channel safely. The tug boat shug shuged. The ship creaked as it was maneuvered along past the wharves and around obstacles.

Alex addressed a few minor problems with the navigation lights and watch schedule to his satisfaction, and they were finally finished with the process of being towed out. The harbor pilot returned to his craft, and Alex then called out the compass course, repeating the numbers loudly. "330." Then, "335." He said the numbers one at a time – three — one — zero and later – "Right twenty."

As they lost sight of the coastline, Alex did one more

check of the forecast to be certain they were unlikely to encounter rough seas and gave control of the deck to his first officer, Max Savoy. She was an ambitious first officer who was planning for an unlimited master's license, which would allow her to operate anywhere in the world. Alex had long ago obtained his unlimited master's license following attendance at Maine Maritime Academy in Castine, and a long series of experiences on board where he moved up the chain of command rather quickly. His father had tutored him in the mechanics and leadership of the profession, so he was ready early in life.

He had graduated from high school early and taken some college courses at the University of Maine, but quickly transferred to the Maritime Academy because he knew what he wanted. That was not what his father had wanted for him, however. They had argued long into some nights, with his mother and sister going to bed and pretending not to notice the tension. His father had invested his earnings and bought land. In addition, he was part owner of a number of fishing vessels and fish processing facilities. He'd branched out even further when there were other investment opportunities available. His son could easily manage some of his investments or farming enterprises. There was enough of his father's earnings generating a comfortable living for his family.

So the last thing his father wanted was for him to sail the seas as a cargo master. He had taught Alex as a way to spend time together. However, Alex was determined from a young age, and his father knew when he was fighting a losing battle. When he realized Alex would not give in, he helped his son to get the best possible education. Alex was first employed on a cargo ship as deck cadet.

He worked his way up to first officer in a few years and was prepared when he applied for the position of master. He was young compared to many who held the position, but his youthful appearance hid a wealth of insight, knowledge and intelligence that he put to good use. Like his father, he invested his earnings and was financially comfortable without having to rely on his family. However, he knew he'd return to some property near them when he was ready to give this up. He considered the long trek to this point in his life as he went to his quarters to unwind. He opened his laptop and sent a quick note to Kara.

Dear Kara, we left the Elizabeth Channel hours ago and have had good weather so far. It will likely take us about ten days to get to Rotterdam if the weather holds. We were treated to a rare show of acrobatics by Blue Whales shortly after we left the coast. I'm attaching a photo shared by one of our crew. I've been thinking about whether you'd like to visit the ship sometime when we return. Wishing you were here,

    Alex

Kara returned to the office after Alex had left for his trip. When she opened her office door and sat down to look over some accounts on her computer, her mind wandered for a moment. She wondered what Alex was doing. The time sped by as she re-engaged in the auditing activity that was so necessary to the companies for which her firm worked. Before she knew it, it was noon and time for lunch. Nita, a friend of Kara's, stood outside her office waiting.

"So, I heard you were out of pocket for a while," she said smiling. "Anything we should know?" Nita was a New Yorker who had lived in the same neighborhood all her life. Her dialect was that of a New Yorker who emphasized the "aw" sound and dropped the "r's" from her words so that "water" became "wada." This was something Kara had grown accustomed to since befriending Nita. She was capable of turning it off since she was the third generation and had mixed with a national and international set. Her family was originally from Puerto Rico, so her words had even more of a twist as she asserted herself among her peers. Nita, a computer tech, was part of Sadie's crowd, but was surprised to learn that Kara worked not far from where she was employed.

"No, busybody, nothing you should know, Nita." She smiled, stood up and turned off the light, grabbed her purse from her desk drawer and walked out with Nita. When they arrived at a delicatessen, they ordered their meal and sat down.

"Someone said they saw you out with this tall, dark handsome..." Nita paused. "But no, it couldn't be you since everybody knows you don't date men."

"Who told you that, Nita?" Kara asked. She pursed her lips as though holding back a secret, looked down and then away.

"Just someone who said you were likely to be a woman's woman instead of a man's woman," Nita said, winking and taking another bite of her sandwich. "So, come on, what's the problem?" she asked, shrugging her shoulders. "Who am I gonna tell?"

"Right, like really, so you're right." Nita began to squirm in her chair. "Alright already," she said. "You can stop with the suspense. Who is he and how did you meet him?"

Kara explained her trip to the ballet and the couple of romantic days she'd spent with Alex. She went on to explain his work and that he was to be out to sea for about a month.

"Knock me ovah with a featha," Nita said. "You been hiding youself from us, girlfriend. Sounds like you found a keepa. You gonna see him again when he gets back?"

"Probably, yes, no, definitely," Kara sighed and wondered whether this was a path she might like to take. He sounded ready to settle down, but she didn't think she wanted to trust a man to be a part of her life. She'd lived so much on her own that she'd found her comfort zone. It wasn't like she really needed to be with a man.

"So we're goin' out tonight. You want to come? We're going to catch a show and then maybe go dancing."

"I don't know, Nita," she said. "I really got behind on something I had planned to do to catch up at work."

"When are you gonna stop giving that company your free labor, girl? It's not like they appreciate it."

"I...yes they do. And, anyway, I might not want to do this for much longer." Nita took a deep breath, and her brown eyes widened.

"You mean to tell me you might quit or something?"

"I don't know. Lately, I've been feeling burned out. Like I want to do something a little different. Maybe open a little boutique or something that doesn't take the level of concentration and intense work that I've been doing for years."

"You can do that? I mean, you got the money to open something like that?"

"I've got a little something put aside for a rainy day," she said. Actually, she'd invested wisely and set aside a great deal of her extra salary, but taxes were high in New York, and she didn't see the point in staying in the state at this rate.

"Well, in that case come on out with us. It can't hurt. You need some time away from your work," Nita said. Kara thought about it for a moment and agreed. They met later that night with some friends.

When she returned home that night, she was surprised at how relaxed she felt in the company of the women that she enjoyed visiting. She wondered whether she'd received an email from Alex and opened her computer. Smiling, she read the email and returned a note to him.

Dear Alex, when you left, I must admit that I needed the time to be with myself. One of the things I didn't tell you is that I grew up in a home with too many people in it. I often rode the bus to the library just to get away from the pandemonium. I guess that's how I got lost in a world of books and numbers. Now, though, I've been thinking I might want a different kind of life. Nita, a friend of mine, and I had lunch today. She was surprised when I confirmed our dates. I'd like to see those Blue Whales too.

Looking forward to hearing from you again,
Kara

CHAPTER FOUR

As the ship traveled farther north, the bitter north winds were evident, so he put on a parka as did the officers and crew. Even though it was mid spring, the northern waters were still quite cold and the breeze from the Arctic whipped through the vessel. The varied colored containers, lashed securely to the ship, sang and cranked as the ship moved through the Atlantic. The crewmembers did their jobs. Most of them were from the Philippines, India or China, pleased to have the salary that merchant charters paid. The upper level crewmembers lived in rooms with a television, full-size bed, refrigerator, shower and tub. Lower level crewmembers had access to some of the same accommodations but with not as spacious environs. Alex, as the master of the ship, had a larger than usual bed, television, refrigerator, desk and meeting area. Besides fulfilling his duties to be certain that every aspect of the ship ran well, his responsibility was for the safety of the crew.

***

When Max was relieved, she went to her cabin to rest. Her short dark blond hair gave her a pixie look when she took off her uniform. But her long legs and firm buttocks made Porter mad with lust. Porter knocked on her door; she opened it quickly to prevent others from hearing them. Porter Williams, as third officer, was due to take the next watch but wanted to see her. He was about her height, and was muscled and firm from using the ship's fitness facilities. His dark good looks gave him a bad boy appearance. He grinned at her, a lock of dark hair falling over his forehead. They had few moments together, but theirs was a relationship of convenience. They knew what each wanted. He stood there, leaning against the door as though waiting for her to give him a signal that it was OK. She smiled. He pushed away from the door and locked it as he watched her unbutton her shirt and slip out of her pants. He licked his lips and unbuckled his belt, zipped his pants down and pulled out his engorged cock. He walked toward her, unbuttoning his shirt.

She smoothed her hands over his muscled chest and down his tight abs while he fingered her clitoris and then slid a finger into her. She moaned.

"I think you're ready for me, puss," he said, smiling. "Come get your cock."

He lifted her on the desk and pushed her legs open. Finding her entrance with his engorged rod, he pushed into her slick wetness. "Baby, you are so good." He gave her a moment to adjust to his size and kissed her lips. He pinched her nipples and took her soft lips into his own. Then he began the slow rhythmic thrust, in out. Her passage felt warm and tight as he pulled in and out of her. He placed a thumb on her clitoris and increased the depth of his thrusts. He could feel her beginning to lose it. She lay back on the desk, rolling her head from side to side.

"That's it baby, give it to me. Give me your sweetness. Let me feel you come," he said. She clenched her teeth and moaned trying not to make too much noise. He bent over her and took her scream into his mouth as she contracted around his shaft. When he felt her orgasm begin, he picked up the pace of his thrusts and held her legs while he plowed into her. He exploded inside her.

"Max, sweet Max, yes," he whispered.

***

On the sixth day of the journey, his first officer came to Alex with a problem. One of the crewmembers had fallen ill. It was difficult to tell whether this was fever caused by something the man had picked up in his home country or whether he fell ill because of something he'd eaten. Alex visited the man's quarters to see what he could do to help, but his second mate already had things under control.

A day away from Rotterdam, he confirmed the arrangements for offloading and checked with his officers about the load and harbor procedures. When everything appeared ready, the ship pulled into Rotterdam's massive harbor, unloaded and was reloaded for a return cargo of containers within eight hours. The process was flawless, too quick by the reckoning of some of his crew, who would like to have visited the port city for its array of entertainment. The harbor officials had boarded and accepted his declaration of passengers. Since the crewmember who had been ill had recovered, he did not report an ill crew member. They were off and headed back to New Jersey before the crew knew what had happened. He was eager to return to the states — to Kara. Two days into the return trip, he wrote to her.

Dear Kara,

As you know, the trip to Rotterdam is fast. We arrived in nine days with little in the way of impediments. One of the ship's crew was ill but recovered under the dutiful care of my second officer. We return for additional containers that will be delivered at a far away port. I doubt if we will be in port for very long as it does not take long for the containers to be loaded. Every minute we waste is money spent by the merchants who pay for this service, so we dare not linger. I hope to see you before we take off. It may be though that I am unable to leave the ship. We will likely be docking at Maher Terminal near Corbin. It may be too much to ask to see you there, but if you wish, ask the car service to bring you to the dock. The ship is called the Emma Ideal. It's a Handymax ship. Tell the harbor officials when you arrive and you should be directed to the ship with little trouble. I've heard from my father about some plans to get involved in the family business. I hope to see you soon.

Love, Alex

Alex hovered over the "send" icon on his email. Signing the letter off with the word "love" was taking a big chance with Kara. He didn't want to scare her into thinking she must make a commitment, but at the same time, he wanted her to know that she was important to him. What the hell, he thought. He clicked "send."

Kara read the email from Alex and closed her laptop. She had gone to a local bookstore to listen to a talk about *The Glass Castle*, by Jennette Walls. The author's frank discussion of her childhood with parents who seemed oblivious to their children helped her to work through feelings about her own parents. She considered the author's circumstances and her own – parents who barely provided adequate food and shelter, or one who provided those necessities but did not seem to observe boundaries. She read Alex's note again and noticed the word "love" this time. Was he using it as a simple closing or did he really mean it? She wondered whether she should make a bold decision.

CHAPTER FIVE

Five days into the return trip, Alex decided to try a telephone call to Kara. With satellite technology on board, it was usually possible to get a call through with no trouble. Just as on land, though, if a storm was nearby, the call could be dropped. It dropped at first, but he tried again. She answered on the fourth ring.

"Kara?"

"Alex? Is that you? Hi." She was surprised that she felt so excited about his call.

"Hey, Kara, how are things going?"

"Fine, Alex, it's good to hear from you. Are you alright? I mean is the ship still going to be here in a few days?"

"Yes, we're right on schedule. I was thinking about you and wondering whether you'd received my email."

"I did," she said. An awkward moment of silence followed. "I, um. I wondered whether you might want some company."

"You mean you'll be there when we dock?"

"Yes, that's my plan. Do you think? Um. I might be making some changes in my life, Alex." Silence. "Alex, are you there?"

"Yes, yes, I'm here. What kind of changes?"

"I think. I'm ready to let go of my job for now. I mean. I think it's time for me to do something different."

"That's good news, sweetheart. I mean. I hope it's good news," he said.

"It's scary. But, I've been thinking about if for some time now. Before I met you I thought about it. I just didn't know what I wanted to do."

"So you've figured out what it's going to be?"

"Um, no, not exactly. I think I'll probably look in Maine for a while."

"Kara, I'm so happy to hear you say that." He balled his fist and pulled a punch as though achieving a victory. Yes.

"I thought maybe I might find an apartment near where you're going to be if you think it won't crowd you too much."

"Yes, I mean no, of course not. I'm looking forward to having you near. This must be a big step for you, Kara. Do you need any help with the move? I have some cousins who would be happy to help you."

"Actually, I'm leasing out my place in Manhattan with the furniture and everything in it for a while. Then, I'll probably move in stages."

"That sounds good," he said. The line began to have static. "I think we're about to lose our connection, Kara, so I've got to hang up. You've made me very happy, Kara. I hope you don't feel this is going to get complicated because it's not."

"OK, I'll talk to you later, Alex," she said. The phone clicked as they lost the connection.

Alex looked at his phone for a moment while he considered what Kara had told him. It might be that things would work out after all. He smiled and got up from his chair.

***

Alex arrived on the navigation bridge in time to check all arrival plans for the trip back to the states. They were about a day away with few problems. The problem with one of the ship's pumps was solved before they departed; however, the ship's mechanics were investigating a possible new pump problem. He checked the reports on the engine room and another about the cargo hold. They were in for a little rough weather, but he had planned to steer around it for the safety of the cargo and crew. He checked the weather report and looked up in time to see Max arrive. She looked as though she had something on her mind, but she wasn't a person who believed in sharing much of her personal life.

"Captain," she said, nodding at him. He nodded back. They weren't as formal as the military but observed some of the same positions and responsibilities. "We noticed that you seem to have some interest in returning post haste to the states. Any reason? I mean, if I might ask."

Alex looked at her, smiled and turned back to the report. Deck cadet Cliff Ledoux looked down at his shoes. The bosun, Toney Cantu, arrived to say that everything was in order below deck. The crew double-checked the load for the swing they planned to make around a bit of rough weather. Already, the ship was beginning to bounce and bob as a result of the high waves caused by the storm. The deck cadet left the bridge.

Second officer Rob Olsen stood at the controls, ready for the captain to give him a new set of coordinates. When they were called out, he made the adjustments and set the ship on a new path. The tension on the bridge lessened a bit as it was clear that the captain wasn't going to take a chance with the load or with the lives of the crew. Max looked out in the distance. She noticed that the captain hadn't answered her question. It wasn't any of her business, so she shook her head a little and busied herself with her duties.

When everyone was clear of the navigation area except Rob, the captain sat in his chair and looked over at Max.

"In answer to your question, yes, Max, there is a good reason for me to get back with due speed," he said. She looked up from the reports on the counter. Rob kept his eyes focused on the navigation controls and out to sea and his hands on the ship's wheel. His job took focus; he rarely lost it.

She stood near the captain as he looked out to sea and then went to check the radar for the storm pattern. He looked up at her as she walked over to get a look as well.

"It looks like we'll avoid the worst of it, captain," she said.

"Yes, that's my plan. If we can come around, we'll find that we've missed the worst of it." He walked to the far side of the viewing windows, out of hearing of Rob. She followed, keeping a discreet distance between them.

"It happens," he said looking out of the side windows, "that I've met someone."

"I'm happy for you, captain," she said, smiling.

"Thanks," he said, rubbing the side of his jaw. "So, it might be that she's at the dock when we tie up. Put her on the ship's manifest as a temporary passenger. She'll board when we reach New Jersey." He gave her a card with Kara's name on it.

Max grinned at him. "Yes, captain," she said. It wasn't often that he shared that much in the way of personal details. They'd shipped out together on many trips, so they shared a little of their lives with one another. She knew of his father's long career on the sea and of their family in Maine. He'd even invited her to their home once when they had a long layover in between jobs. She could tell that his parents were hoping that something might develop between them, but they were just friends, in a job that required utter attention to details and concentration. It was hard enough for a woman to work her way up the ladder. She was almost there and didn't plan to blow it by starting something she really didn't want. Besides, the sparks weren't there like they were with Porter.

However, this new person in the captain's life was quite different. She knew he planned to retire soon, so maybe this was the beginning of a new life for him. It meant that she might have a better chance of becoming captain, or master of the ship.

She wondered what Porter would say when he heard the news. The captain was professional in his interaction with the officers and crew. Occasionally, he ordered a field day, where the crew got involved in cleaning the ship. It might be that he would want this to be done. So she anticipated his order and asked that the preparations begin for a general spiff up of the ship. Generally, the crew kept things running well, so there wouldn't be much to do. She smiled as she returned to the bridge.

When they pulled into port, the cargo for their trip to Singapore took less time to load than Alex thought it would. He was busy making preparations for the departure when he thought of Kara. Apparently, she hadn't made it to the terminal. So he gave the idea a mental shove. He'd write to her to say he was sorry they'd missed one another. The arrival and turn around had to be smooth and without problems. The one hitch in this trip might be that the manager sent a security team along. It was expensive enough to make this trip, but sending a security team to fend off pirates was more than he could stomach.

Security specialists tended not to answer to anyone. The head security specialist, Jonas Steelman, checked in with him on the starboard side of the ship as he was winding up a check of the lashing of cargo. He'd sent one of the crew members off to send for the chief engineer. He gave Steelman a hard look. The man was tall and muscled. His dark hair and day's growth of beard suggested someone who didn't work to look tough, but was in fact just that.

The man wore a long slicker, which probably hid his weapons. But none of those were in evidence. He wondered whether they would get through the trip without conflict.

"Captain," Steelman said. "We've been given quarters and will stand watch throughout the voyage."

"This is no voyage, Steelman," he said. "But welcome aboard anyway. Just so you know, your crew answers to me."

"No, we answer to the owners of this shipment, sir. We understand you're the master of the ship, but I'm master of my crew and will do anything necessary to protect this shipment and your crew. Without your crew the shipment can't get to where it's going. It's our job."

Alex sighed and looked the man in the eye. He was as tall as Steelman and as broad of shoulder and build. Still, he knew that this wasn't the time to engage in a conflict. The ship was about to put to sea and there were other things needing a check before they left.

"I don't have time for this now, Steelman," he said. "The ship is due to leave port within the next hour. If you can't accept my authority aboard this ship, you're welcome to take your crew and get off before we leave the berth." He pushed past Steelman and walked toward the chief engineer, who had a report about the faulty pump.

After all was done for the departure and the ship was finally on its way, Alex gave over the helm to his second officer and headed for his quarters. He pushed open the door to his cabin to find his bed occupied. He frowned and walked over to the bed, thinking one of Steelman's crew must have mistaken his quarters for an available room. He grabbed the covers and ripped them off the unsuspecting seaman. But it wasn't a seaman at all. It was a woman. He breathed deeply, his heart beating a tattoo in his chest. Her curves looked familiar. She turned over slowly and looked up at him, blinking.

"Alex?"

"Kara? Kara! You're here! I mean. The ship is underway. There's no way to get off."

"I don't plan to get off." She stretched and yawned. Alex stood frozen in place, awestruck at his good luck, his cock stirring to the movement of her body. The noise of the ship receded as he focused on her. She sat up and kneeled in profile. He hardened at the sight of her lush bottom. She reached for him. It took only seconds for him to throw his hat at an odd sculpture on his desk, unzip his pants, unbutton his shirt and slip under the covers with her. She was already undressed, a sweet present for him. He snuggled up to her, enveloping her in his arms as his hardened cock brushed her thighs.

"I've missed you so much," he whispered. "I'm going to show you how much." He began to kiss her, long and deep, moving one hand down her neck and to the tips of her breasts. He lowered his head and sucked on the nipples, swirling his tongue around one and then the other. Then, he reached to her mons, where he fingered her clitoris. She threw back her head. "Alex! Oh. That feels so good. Mmmm. Let me." As he continued his ministrations to her mons, she grabbed him by the shoulders and ran her hands down the flat planes of his stomach till she reached his rod. She wrapped her soft hand around his cock and gave it a gentle tug. He grunted. "I can't wait, Kara; sweetheart, if you continue." He hovered over her, used one knee to spread her legs apart and positioned his swollen penis at the entrance of her slit. He nudged at her and then pushed again. She gasped. "Hold me, sweetheart." She wrapped her arms around him and he surged into her. She was tight and wet as he seated himself deeply inside her.

He pulled back and kissed her again and again, on her lips, her forehead, her nose, her cheeks, her neck. She laughed, full of the joy of their union.

"Kara, I can't last much longer," he said. "You feel so

wonderful." She squeezed him with the muscles of her vagina. His head jerked back and he hissed. "How did you learn to do that?" She grinned. "Sweet candy girl," he said and began moving rhythmically, in out, in out. Soon, the electric pulse of their movement overcame her and she could feel herself losing control, her mouth watered and her eyes became moist as the walls of her channel contracted around his generous cock. As his desire for her exploded, he could feel her flower grasp and release his shaft. It was too much. He pulled back and surged forth again and again, the heavy sack of his scrotum slapping against her buttocks as he stroked her.

Kara felt herself building to another orgasm as he pressed into her. As the second mind tingling zenith arrived, she heard Alex roar, and then release his juice inside her, while uttering a smattering of incoherent words into her ear. He rested on top of her for a while. He rolled off her and stared at the ceiling of his quarters. Panting, he looked at her and smiled. She smiled back, inhaling and exhaling as though she'd run a marathon.

He gathered her in his arms and they slept for a short while. When he woke, he walked to his bathroom, washed and then got a warm cloth for her. He wiped her cleft of the copious fluid he'd deposited. She'd fallen asleep too and woke to his touch. "That was wonderful, Kara," he said as they regained their equilibrium. "I don't think I have a brain cell left." She caressed his face. He returned to the bed and got under the covers with her.

"Kara, sweetheart," he said.

"Ummm."

"You do realize that you're headed for Singapore?"

"Yes."

"Did you intend to stay aboard? Because we don't stop again until we reach South Africa."

"Look in the corner of your room." He turned his head and noticed some luggage.

"You planned this?" he looked astonished.

"As if I can't buy a ticket. Of course I did."

"But, I didn't see your name."

"I did it at the last minute, but I emailed someone about it, a Max Savoy, and made all the arrangements. He didn't tell you?"

Alex pondered the thought for a moment. He had told Max to expect Kara, but perhaps she had misunderstood his intentions. He wanted to visit with Kara, but taking her to Singapore was much too dangerous. While this would be his last job with this charter company, he knew that there were always risks. There could be pirates or a storm, any number of dangers might exist. A cargo ship could get boring for a young woman who was accustomed to living on land.

"I don't want to seem ungrateful Kara, because I. I mean, I'm happy you're here, but there are risks to this leg of the journey."

"I realize that," she said. "I take full responsibility for the risks."

"Kara, sweetheart, you don't realize what kind of 'risks' I mean. This isn't a pleasure cruise. This is a cargo ship. The risks are real and involve lives, your life. I didn't want that to be..." He paused and exhaled, running a hand through his thick hair. "It's just. I don't want anything to happen to you."

"I know, Alex. I appreciate that. But it's my life. I took the risk because I wanted this. My life has been all about not taking risks. So, for once, I decided to take a risk — on you." He smiled and caressed her face with one hand. He pulled her to him and kissed her long and deep. She began to feel the stirrings of arousal in the folds of her center. Blood rushed to her abdomen as he placed a finger on her clitoris. "Alex," she said throatily. "Alex, please."

He kissed her on her breasts, down her arms and stomach and spread her legs, descending on her pubis. He lapped at the swollen lips. She tasted so sweet and salty, he couldn't get enough of her. He worked his way up the lips of her labia until he found her hardened clitoris and placed it between his lips. He rolled it between his lips, flicking it with his tongue again and again. Soon, she felt herself coming again, the contractions so strong, she felt like she was floating. She felt light and feathery as the spasms continued. He rose from her and picked her up and turned her around so her ass faced him. She was slick and wet. He probed her with his cock, once, twice. Pushing in and pulling out. He could hear the wet sounds of sliding in and out of her sweet cleft.

He then sank deep inside her and set up a steady rhythm. He held her buttocks with both hands and thrust his rod deep inside her. He could feel his own orgasm hurtling out of his cock. "Kara! Sweet Kara! Yes," he shouted, thrusting once twice then stilling as he came, his jism spurting deep into her sweet, juicy love channel.

They slept long and deep then. When Alex came to, it was dark and he thought to check with his first and second mates. He checked the cameras on his computer. All seemed quiet. Still, he found himself concerned; he showered, dressed and went to the bridge where Max was on watch.

"Max," he said, looking over the computer charts and checking the weather. "Everything on course?"

"Yes, captain, all is well." A tense silence seemed to be on the bridge.

"Max," Alex said. "I'd like to have a word with you in the officer's room."

"Yes, captain," she said. "Ten minutes?"

He nodded. He went to the officer's area to make himself a cup of coffee and to check on the general state of affairs for the visiting security team. He was talking to a deck cadet when Max walked in. The deck cadet could tell that there would be a discussion and made himself scarce.

Alex stirred his own coffee and offered a cup to Max. She took it from him and poured cream and sugar in hers. He began to drink his, black, and leaned against the counter.

"Max, I understand you received an email from Ms. Carlisle indicating that she planned to join us. Why didn't you inform me?"

"I thought you knew. I...You gave me her name. I thought you planned for her to be aboard."

"The idea was for her to visit, not to remain on board ship," he said, grimacing. Silence. She looked into her cup as though there were answers for her there. She swallowed, her mouth going dry, and shifted her weight.

"We get passengers every now and then, so I didn't think it was a problem. She paid the fare and received the information about the risks and the route. I thought it would be a good thing."

"You thought it would be a good thing," he said, smiling and then he chuckled and then laughed. "A good thing... Did it occur to you that the threat of pirates and other dangers might make it a good 'thing' for you to tell me about this particular passenger?"

"I looked for you as we were loading, captain, but actually after I showed her to your quarters. Um. I assumed that was OK?"

He looked down then into her face. She was a bit shorter than him, but not by much.

"Yes, it was alright to put her in my quarters, but you should have told me she was aboard."

"I tried to find you, but there was so much to do. We were trying to get out on time, so I sort of forgot about her after I showed her to your quarters. She must have fallen asleep or something. She looked tired when I left her there. So I figured she wanted to nap. I told her that you'd check in on her soon. She didn't seem worried." She spoke rapidly when she was nervous.

"It's OK, Max," he said. "Relax, she's where she's

supposed to be. It's just that I wish I'd known. So do we have a stowaway?"

"No, captain, I put her name on the list of passengers that we reported to the harbor patrol."

"Well that's something good out of all this, I suppose," he said. "In future, let me know whenever someone like her boards the ship. Uh, what I mean is when she boards. Or. Never mind. I think you know what I mean." Max smiled, knowing there was something special about this woman.

"Yes, captain." She looked away toward the outer corridor as though she were looking for someone to come through the door.

"That's all, Max. Let's try to make our unexpected passenger comfortable."

"Yes sir," she said. She began to walk away.

"Max," he said. "I also want you to keep an eye on that security team the company sent. I want to know if they so much as sneeze wrong."

"Yes, sir," she said and made a hasty exit.

CHAPTER SIX

The days on board a cargo ship were not a vacation for those who worked on it, but when the duty shift was over and it was time to relax, there were plenty of diversions for the crew. In addition, plenty of food and beverages were available. When Kara woke, it was morning. She showered and dressed. Alex seemed to have been gone for some time. The sheets on his side of the bed were cool. She vaguely recalled his having risen and dressed, but was too tired to register it all. She dressed in a pair of jeans and an orange tunic. She swept her hair into a ponytail and put on some lip balm. Her skin looked as though she'd tanned for some time. She seldom worried about further makeup. As she pulled her tunic down and gave her hair one more assessing look in the mirror, someone knocked. She opened the door. A woman a bit taller than her stood in the doorway. She was muscled and lean. She wore her hair short. She held out her hand to Kara. She was dressed in khaki slacks and the white twill shirt of a uniform.

"Hi, I'm Max, the first mate on board this tank," she said. Kara smiled and shook hands with Max. The woman seemed to be open and friendly.

"I'm Kara. I think we met, right? You showed me to the captain's quarters."

"That's right. But I didn't have time to get acquainted with you then." She paused, looking past Kara to her luggage.

"I see you're getting settled in."

"Yes, um, come on in. I was just about to go in search of something to eat," said Kara. Max stepped into the door and shut it behind her.

"That's good because part of my mission is to make certain you know where to find things. Ordinarily, one of the crew members would be assigned this, but since I'm, since we're." She paused again. They both smiled and then laughed. "Look, a place like this can get lonely if you don't have friends, so I thought I might help you get to know the place a little. You ready?"

Kara nodded and they left the confines of the captain's cabin to explore the ship. Max took Kara first to the officer's eating area. She was served breakfast while Max went to do a few chores. Max returned in about 30 minutes to share pastry with Kara and a cup of coffee. When they finished, Max showed her the recreation facilities, complete with exercise equipment such as weights and treadmills, rowing machines and a ping pong table. There was also an area where the crew could play court sports such as badminton and tennis. An additional recreational area featured a large-screen television, where the crew watched films, played chess and other games. A bar included a number of chairs in a comfortable, carpeted setting. It was clear that the crew used this area to socialize, drink and try their hand at karaoke.

After the tour of the recreational areas, Max left Kara on the deck of the ship, having explained the importance of staying away from the containers and the railings. If there was a sudden shift, a person could easily go overboard, she said.

As Kara stared out at the vast ocean she heard a familiar voice behind her. Kyle Fenwick had dated her in the early days of her time in New York. He had tried everything he could think of to get her in bed. But it was the early days for her then; she was freshly delivered from her family, by herself, and not wanting intimacy. For Kara, it was about escaping relationships. She wasn't about to trap herself with a man who could be very much like her stepfather. Kyle's good looks were part of what attracted her to him, but he was much too pushy. While he wasn't violent, she sometimes felt that the potential for violence was under the surface. When he had groped her after a date, she decided it was too much and refused to see him any longer. She turned around just as two men came through a door on the side of the ship.

Kyle looked at her as if he'd seen a ghost. He stopped in his tracks. "Kara!" he exclaimed. "What are you doing here?"

"I could ask the same of you, Kyle," she said. She wanted to smile, but the urge didn't come, so she didn't force herself to do so. They stood there for a few seconds before Kyle launched into a nervous explanation and introduction. He explained that he was part of the security team sent to protect the containers. He introduced the man with him, Jonas Steelman, who was looking at her as though she were a delectable desert that he was ready to eat up. She explained that she was a passenger. She eased her way toward to door to try to get away from them. They made small talk about the weather, the crew and the quality of the ship. Just as she was about to turn toward the door, she heard Alex.

"Steelman," he said, nodding and giving both men a cold stare. He placed a protective and possessive hand on Kara's shoulder. Both men stood rigidly, having realized that Kara was the captain's woman. "Kara," he said as he pulled her through the door. "I thought you were going to stay in my quarters for the rest of the day." He said it loud enough for the two men to hear so that they understood that she was with him. Realizing that this was mostly for show, she picked up on his proprietary ruse by saying just as loudly, "I was waiting for you to return when Max gave me a tour." There, it should be clear enough now to both men that she wasn't interested or available.

When they got to his quarters, Alex pulled her into his arms and kissed her deeply. He unzipped her stretchy jeans and rolled them down her legs, slipping off her athletic shoes. He then pulled off her panties, a pair of red bikinis that made him twitch to bury himself in her sweet depths. He placed a finger in her opening and worked it in and out. Her creamy scent overpowered him; she smelled like oranges and cinnamon. He lifted her on to his desk and gently bent each of her legs so her feet rested on the edge of the desk. He couldn't get enough of her. He unzipped his own pants and let them pool around his legs, pulled out his engorged cock and placed it at her entrance. He thrust inside her, then placed his hands under her buttocks and helped her wrap her legs around him. Then the real fun began; he pulled out of her and surged into her again and again.

"Alex!" she gasped holding tight to him. "Yes! Yes!" Her throaty voice called to him.

He could feel her beginning to come as he maintained his rhythm, thrusting with such force that the desk upon which he held her began to vibrate. He felt himself lose his seed in her sweet canal as they both panted with spent joy. He gingerly pulled her up and reached down to pull up his pants. Then, he picked her up and carried her to the bed. They lay in one another's arms for an hour before he got up, washed and checked the monitors on his computer. She yawned and stretched as he turned back to her.

"Are you OK?" he asked. "I know I was a little overeager there."

"I'm OK," she said, smiling. "I think I want to get some more rest."

"That's a good idea, Kara; you've had a lot going on." He turned back to the computer and checked a few more details from his chief engineer. They would be coming near the coast of Nigeria in a few days.

"Kara," he said, turning back to her again. He sat on the bed with her and took her hand in his. "Try to stay away from that security team. You seemed like you knew them."

"I do. I mean. I know one of them. Kyle Fenwick. We dated briefly when I first came to New York."

"I thought you only hung out with women."

"I do. I did. But I met Kyle early in my time in New York."

"What happened?"

"Oh, nothing. I just didn't want to see him anymore. He was a little too…" she didn't finish the sentence, but looked toward the covered window. "I just."

"Look, you don't have to explain. But, if either one of them or anyone at all looks at you wrong, I want to know about it."

"What do you mean by that?" she asked frowning. "Everybody has been polite to me. I haven't noticed anything out of the ordinary."

"I know. You wouldn't with my crew. They answer to me. They're my team and wouldn't do anything to harm or frighten you. But the security team answers to a different authority. They are still part of my charge, but the tension about who answers to whom is going to increase in the next few days."

"Why?"

"Soon, we'll enter waters where pirates are common. I'm trying to steer a course as far away from them as possible without losing time, but it might be that they still find us. If that happens, the security details might cause more trouble for us. Things could get a little dicey. I want you to stay in my quarters as much as possible beginning tomorrow night. Everything should go fine, but just in case."

"What do you mean by 'dicey'?" she asked.

"Violent." She took a deep breath. Violence was something Kara always tried to stand firmly against. Having been on the receiving end of it as a child, she had trouble accepting any form of violence for any reason. She knew that in some cases it took violence to subdue someone who could cause harm to innocents, but she reasoned that there were always alternatives. She grimaced, looked down then up at Alex.

"Is there anyway to avoid that sort of thing? I mean." She twisted her hands, which had become sweaty. "Isn't it possible to avoid that situation altogether?"

Alex closed his laptop and placed his hat on top of the computer. His broad shoulders and narrow hips making a delicious tableau as Kara eyed him. She felt a tug at her core as she perused him. He smiled as though he knew what she was thinking. However, his face then went blank as though he were considering business.

"Kara, this is a cargo ship. We will have some protection from the U.S. Navy, but the owners of the shipment have hired a security team as added insurance. We can't know what might happen. But know this. I'll be sure you're protected. In order to do my job and protect you and the crew, I need to know you're safe."

"But what about the violence? Does that mean guns? What might happen?"

"It could mean guns, knives, all manner of possibilities," he said. He walked to her and sat down on the bed. He held her shoulders and kissed her, feathering his lips over hers then pressing them as though he was ready to lay her down. He pulled back as though he had come to his senses. He shook his head. His hands cupped her face and he looked into her eyes. "Kara, keep the door locked when I'm not here." He took a deep breath. "No one's likely to try anything, but just to be on the safe side, stay here as much as possible. I know you'll get cabin fever from time to time and need to walk about, go to the gym maybe. But try to wait until I can be with you. I've asked Max to look out for you too."

"I don't need a keeper or a chaperone, Alex," she said. "I don't want to feel like I'm being watched."

"You're not being watched, sweetheart. You're being kept safe." He walked back to the desk and pulled out a paper map. "Here, I want you to understand what's at stake and what we're doing." He spread the map out between them. He pointed to a place on the map. "Here's where we are, just about. We're far enough away from Nigeria to avoid any conflict. But there could be pirates looking for cargo this far out. We're going to try to outmaneuver them. It may mean getting near the shore and then taking an unexpected route. That's a hard thing to do for a ship this size. But, we're going to try to stay out of their way." He traced a line to South Africa. "We'll stop in South Africa briefly, then go on toward Singapore. That part of the trip is risky as well. But we may have the benefit of more naval protection close by."

"Is there anything I can do?" she said looking up at him. "I can use a gun."

"What! You're kidding, right?"

"No, I'm not kidding. I can use a gun. I took a class in college on a lark."

He looked in her eyes and pulled her close to him. "Sweetheart, if I do my job properly, you won't have to think about using a gun. But I'm happy to know that you're not frightened of them and know how to use one." He walked over to his locker and pulled out a case — a set of guns nestled in canvas lining. "These are kept in my locker. If you think you need one of them, this is how they work." He demonstrated the use of basic safety mechanisms, bullets and firing aspects. He took a look at her, shook his head as though he had a hard time believing she could use a weapon and put the case away.

"Are there any more surprises you have in store for me?" he asked.

"Now that you ask, I do know a little self-defense." He smiled.

"Good, that's a good thing for any woman to know." He pulled her too him and kissed her on the forehead. "Kara," he said. "Marry me." She gasped and looked up at him.

"Are you serious?"

"Yes, why wouldn't I be?"

"No," she said.

"Why not?"

"You don't love me, Alex. You just want me because…" she paused and looked toward the windows. "Maybe I'm convenient."

"Is this what this is about? You think I can't be in love with you? This can't be love?"

"Alex, men, people don't fall in love with each other in such a short amount of time. Besides, why can't we just go along the way we have been without marriage?"

"Are you saying this because of your parents' marriage, Kara? Because not all families are like yours was. Ours can be good." Silence. She pulled away from him and walked to the window. She pulled the curtain back and looked out. One of the crewmembers walked by without looking their way. She let the curtain fall into place. The ocean stretched out beyond the window.

"I don't want to commit to a marriage. I just don't want to be trapped like that. I'm not ready. What I mean is…I do want to be with you, but just not like that." He walked over to the window and turned her around.

"I just want you to know that not all men are like your stepfather, Kara. We can have a good marriage and a happy family. But if you need time, I can understand that. I just want you to be happy." He fumbled in his back pocket and pulled out a silver ring. It had entwined ropes on it. Her eyes widened. He smiled. He picked up her left hand and placed it on her ring finger. "Just for this trip, would you mind wearing my ring? It's not an engagement ring. It just means that you're thinking about it. Besides which, it might keep you safe."

"Where did you get this, Alex?"

"It's just a little something I picked up while you weren't looking." He grinned. "Just hold on to it for me. Promise me you'll at least consider staying with me for the next, say, a couple of years or so." She smiled. She held out her hand and looked at the ring.

"So this is the "think-about-it" ring," she said grinning. "That doesn't sound too bad. I can work with that." She held up her index finger. "But no promises. I want to think about it first." He grinned.

"It's a deal then. The 'think-about-it' ring is good for as long as you need it. Think about it as long as you like." He gave her hug and held her at arm's length. "Now, I have to get to work. Enjoy yourself for the next day or so. I'll let you know when you need to stay indoors."

He walked to the door. "And don't forget to lock the door behind me."

CHAPTER SEVEN

The next day was focused on preparation. Alex had taken this route before. He had a friend in the Nigerian Navy and had emailed him of his intentions to navigate near the coast as they left Nigerian waters. He hoped that this might help him find a way to skirt any potential risk. Later, his second mate, Rob Olsen, sighted some activity some distance from the stern of the ship.

"What do you think's going on there, Rob?" he asked. Other officers and crewmembers were also at the bridge assisting with the complicated tasks required to get the ship to its destination. He sent a text to Kara warning her to stay in his cabin. She affirmed that she'd received his message.

"It's clear they're up to no good, capain," Rob said. "They're trying to appear like a ship in distress, but they're moving too fast now." Rob looked through binoculars, scanning the horizon. "Looks like there might be two, capain."

"Max, send a distress signal to all ships in our area," Alex said. "Make it clear that we're under attack. Don't wait. Send it now."

"Aye aye, captain," she said and put out the message to all ships.

Alex had gone through the credentials of his crew long ago to get some notion of which ones had some experience with weapons. While asking his crew to be prepared for trouble was not what he wanted to do, he thought it only fair to let them know. Many ships had had crewmembers taken and held for ransom because they were simply not prepared to resist. He held regular meetings with his officers to have them initiate training to resist pirates. Some simple precautions and a show of force sometimes helped.

Two small craft were behind them, approaching with caution, but steadily gaining on the Emma Ideal; he sent an alert to the crew to be on guard. The extent to which they wished to arm themselves was left to their discretion. However, enough of a warning had been issued. Jonas Steelman, ever vigilant during the journey, sent his men to the stern. They were already armed and ready to defend the ship. Alex pulled Steelman aside for a word.

"We're certain that this small craft is a pirate vehicle. However, alert your men that the Nigerian Navy could respond as well. We don't want to fire on the wrong vessel," he said, giving Steelman a cold look. "As soon as they get within range fire at will."

Steelman nodded and headed for the stern. The small craft had made its way to the side of the ship and was firing in the air. Many pirates knew that captains would stop the ship rather than risk an explosion or damage to their cargo. However, Alex had given orders for the ship to continue at full throttle. He could hear gunshots on the starboard side.

He had placed a secondary case of weapons on the bridge and ordered it opened so that all could arm themselves. He grabbed his own gun and two other weapons. "Steady and leeward, Rob, full throttle. Hold her." Rob nodded. He left the bridge and made progress to the starboard side. He saw several men trying to make their way on board. However, Steelman and his crew were picking them off. The pirates were a diverse lot. They included not only Africans, but also European and Asian men. They seemed to know the ship as though it were second nature. Alex crossed to the port side of the ship where the pirates had another vessel. It appeared that some were making progress up the side of the ship.

He picked off the two who made it over the side of the ship and pushed them overboard. He wondered whether any had made it to the crew accommodation deck. He glanced at the Monkey Island and noticed a pirate had made it to the area where radio transmissions were sent. He had to take a chance to shoot the man off the island. He aimed carefully and shot true. The man fell on the deck below. Alex spied the grappling hooks hanging from the side of the ship. Using a special device, he worked two of them free. He was able to get another free using a tool on board. He worked to get those free and went to the starboard side to do the same there.

Alex pulled out one more weapon from his sling. This one was certain to make it impossible for the vessel below to continue to send assailants on board. He aimed and fired. The weapon, much like a bazooka, fired into the vessel and created a small explosion. The boat began to take on water. Alex saw men scrambling about the vessel to try to salvage it, but soon they realized it was too late. As he turned to see to the other vessel, he heard a shot within the crew accommodation area. The hair on the back of his neck stood on end. Kara!

CHAPTER EIGHT

Kara had just returned from the mess room and closed the door behind her when she heard shots. She locked the door and backed away from it, her eyes getting round and her hands shaking. She listened, turning her head this way and that as she heard gunshots and the shouts of people screaming in pain. She tried to compose herself, but memories of violence came surging forth. She remembered the sounds of leather hitting objects and hitting human skin, her skin, the skin of her siblings. She shivered and sank to her knees. "No!" she shouted. "No!" She held her hands to her ears to try to block out the sound. But the sound of the shots and voices of people fighting for their lives assailed her senses. She balled up into a fetal position and held herself, the sound of each shot causing her to flinch in pain.

Then, she heard the sound of the door rattling. Someone was trying to get into the room – someone who shouldn't be here. Someone must have heard her shouting. She unfurled and leapt to the locker where Alex kept his guns. She dragged the case out to the floor and opened it. The door handle continued to rattle and the door began to shake. Someone knew she was here.

Her hands shook as she checked to see that the gun was

loaded. She stood and pointed the gun at the door. Her hand trembled as she aimed. She took a deep breath. The door gave way in one violent burst as the man behind it shoved his shoulder into it. A tall, heavy man stood there, his face partially obscured by a hat. When he saw her, he motioned for her to give him the gun. He licked his lips and grabbed his crotch with one hand. He reached for her, while rubbing himself. She trembled. The gun shook in her hands. Time seemed to freeze. Kara tried to remember that she was no longer a helpless child. She focused her mind and backed away from the man. His arrogant posture suggested that he knew he could take the gun away from her easily.

Kara could hear the struggles of other crew members down the hall. He stepped closer to her. "Stop," she said. "I. . . I don't want to shoot you. Stop!" He stepped toward her to grab the gun. She fired. His eyes grew large; he smiled and reached for her again, but then fell back, like a tall tree that someone had cut down. She pulled back from him and dropped the gun. Her mouth was dry, and her heart beat wildly. She felt nauseous and dizzy. She could hear the sounds of grunting as though someone was fighting in the hall. She picked the gun up and stepped over the body. When she stepped into the hallway, she could see Max fighting what looked to be a pirate.

She held the gun limply in one hand. She wanted the confusion to stop for the noise to stop. She wanted to place her hands over her ears, but the gun was in her hand. She looked down at it. It seemed heavy. She grabbed it with both hands and brought it up. "Stop! No! Stop or I'll shoot. Stop now! Stop!" she screeched. Max and the man moved about so quickly that she was afraid she'd hit Max instead of the man. She was about to fire the weapon when someone grabbed her from behind in a chokehold. A man who smelled like fish and gunpowder knocked the gun from her hand and began to drag her back. Her vision clouded as she watched the fading forms of Max and the man engaged in a fight. Max seemed to be winning, but Kara was losing consciousness as she fought for air. The man picked her up and flung her over his shoulder. She was able to breathe again, but stars appeared before her eyes. She could see he was about to go through a door to the open deck. That couldn't happen. She tried to clear her head.

As the man tried to get through the door, she grabbed the sides of it and held on. The force of her movement jerked them both to the floor. He landed on top of her. As they struggled to untangle themselves, he grabbed her arms to regain control of her. She kicked at his crotch. He winced in pain. She scrambled away, but as she crawled toward the gun he grabbed her leg and pulled her to him. Then she heard a shot. The man collapsed with his hand still on her ankle. She pulled away from him and scrambled toward the cabin she shared with Alex. She tried to slam the door, but the body of the dead man she'd shot was in the way. Suddenly, all of it was too much for her; everything went black and she sunk to the floor.

Alex climbed over the dead man's body and saw Kara crawling toward his cabin. She appeared to be in shock. He could see in her retreating form a desperation and a panic that seemed to overwhelm her. Max had dispatched two pirates at the far end of the hall; she then was coolly dragging one of them out of the way and toward another door where she received help heaving the dead man over the side of the ship. He pulled another dead man out of the way and went to his cabin. Inside, he saw Kara curled up, rocking on her haunches, and on the floor nearby, a dead body was on the floor. He grimaced, knowing that this would be a hurdle for Kara. He dragged the body out into the hall. Then he picked Kara up and laid her on the bed. She had shut her eyes tight as though doing so would make it all go away.

He kissed her forehead and whispered. "Stay here,

sweetheart. It's not over yet. Stay inside. Don't open the door. I'll be back soon." She groaned and twisted as though she wanted to open her eyes but couldn't. He turned and walked to the door, activated the lock and pulled it tightly shut. The door latch had been broken, so he would have to send someone to repair it. He picked up the dead body and walked to the deck. He threw the man overboard, then walked back to the other pirate and dispatched him as well.

He walked to the bridge to check on the ship. "Hey Rob, any damage?"

"Nothing major, captain."

"How is our security team making out?"

"It looks like two of them are injured, but no one fatally. So far, looks like all crew are onboard with a few injuries."

"Let's check on the ship, Rob. Porter, you take the helm." He nodded and took over. "We need to be sure all unauthorized personnel are off the ship and that there are no grappling hooks or bombs." The two walked through the ship for about 30 minutes checking on its security and making certain all invaders were dispatched. As they re-entered the bridge, Porter nodded.

"Captain, we're in radio contact with the Nigerian Navy. We've sighted a ship astern. We're not sure of the ship's identity. It could be the Navy, but it's too soon to tell. They're moving at about 30 knots...That should put them here in about 30 minutes."

"Let me know when you get a visual confirmation. Rob, take the helm." Rob nodded.

Max came inside the navigation room. She was covered in blood. Porter took one look at her and opened the cabinet to see to her wounds. Alex decided all was in hand here.

"Maintain speed, Rob. We want to get as far away from these bastards as possible."

"Aye aye, captain." Rob punched in the necessary

information; they could see the carnage of the pirates' boats in the rear. He grabbed a billy club on his way out the door.

Alex checked on Kara at his cabin and saw that she seemed to be resting. Sleep was probably the best thing for her. He walked into the room and brushed hair from her forehead. She moaned and turned in her sleep. He found a blanket and covered her, kissed her on the cheek and turned to walk out the door, securing it as he left.

He walked out to the starboard side of the ship to check with Jonas. He and his crew had also dumped bodies overboard. He helped one of the security crew to get a grappling hook overboard when he saw another vessel approaching from the starboard side of the ship. He could make out the flags and could tell that it was a Nigerian Navy patrol boat, but at least one of the security team didn't seem to understand that. Two of the team began to prepare to fire.

"Don't shoot! That's the Nigerian Navy," Alex shouted. One of security team didn't seem to hear and was about to fire when Alex got to him and used the billy club to knock the man to the ground by hitting him behind the knees. He grabbed the gun the man was holding and unloaded it. He threw it to the ground.

"Not every black man you see is the enemy! Use your head!" he shouted.

Alex glared at Jonas. "Get your crew under control," he snapped. "Or I'll do it for you." Jonas walked to his man and held out a hand to help the man up.

"Stand down," Jonas said to his crew. The patrol boat hailed the Emma Ideal and it slowed down. Rob knew what to do, Alex thought. There was no need to tell him. He'd traveled these waters many times and knew friend from foe. They let down a makeshift ladder for boarding and the first face Alex recognized was Nnakeme Imo. A few more men accompanied him. Alex approached him and they shook hands.

"Alex, my friend," Nnakeme said. "I see you have had a bit of trouble."

"We have indeed," Alex said. "However, we took care of the problem."

"I'm sorry we couldn't get to you before now. My orders are to arrest any surviving pirates. Do you have any wounded who need assistance?"

"No, we seem to be in good shape. There were no surviving attackers. Would you like to join me for some refreshment before you return to your vessel?" Alex asked. That was code for whiskey. Nnakeme grinned. They walked to the officer's mess, and Alex broke out a bottle of fine whiskey. He poured a glass for himself and then one for Nnakeme.

"How have you been, my friend?" Alex asked. "When last I saw you, your wife was expecting another child."

"She has given birth. I am now the proud father of another boy. That now makes three girls and two boys." Alex grinned.

"Congratulations. Pictures?" he asked. Nnakeme pulled out his cell phone and showed Alex pictures of his family. Alex smiled as he looked at the photos and wondered whether he would have this sort of family life in the future. He thought of Kara, alone in his room. He needed to get back to her.

"You're a fortunate man, Nnakeme," he said, handing back the phone.

"When are you going to settle down yourself, my friend?" Nnakeme asked. Alex's lips turned up in a tight-lipped smile.

"I'm working on it."

"You will tell me when have success," Nnakeme grinned.

"I will." The two men shared another drink and then parted company.

CHAPTER NINE

The door to his cabin was still battered and unlocked as he entered. He'd have to have Wheeler fix it for him later. He pulled his desk to the door to keep it closed. Alex placed a cold cloth on Kara's head. Her eyes opened, fluttering as she tried to make out who he was. Her face was blank as though she didn't recognize him. She swung wildly at him as though she were in a fight. He grabbed her wrists and held her. "Shhh. It's me, Kara. It's Alex. It's all over. Shhh. Sweetheart." He pulled her to him and held her close, soothing her by running a hand down her back and over her head. He rocked her gently. She began to realize where she was and sobbed. Tears rolled from her eyes as she realized the violence she'd experience. At first, she thought it must have been a dream, but then noticed the blood stains on the floor. She began to shiver.

"Kara, sweetheart, I know you've had a terrible shock."

"Shock!" she shouted. "I killed a man! I killed someone! I shot. I shot." She began to tremble. He held her again.

"Kara, I know this seems bad, but if you hadn't shot him, you would be dead yourself or a hostage. You probably wouldn't have been seen for sometime. Maybe not ever. You did what anyone would do. You not only saved your own life but you probably saved someone else who might have suffered if you hadn't shot." He pulled back and put a hand under her chin. "Sweetheart, if you hadn't shot him, I might never have seen you again. Do you realize what men do to women who are captured under these circumstances? We might have gotten you back after paying a high ransom, but you wouldn't be the same person." She took a deep breath and held him tight.

He held her for a while as she sobbed, then, lowered her to the bed. He took her cloths off, removing first her blouse and then her jeans. She lay on the bed as though she had no energy. He brought a warm wet cloth and a bowl of water and began to sponge her clean. He wiped gently and then used a hand towel to dry her. He took a quick shower himself and dried himself with a towel. He could tell that she needed to be close to him. So he removed his towel and got under the covers with her. He held her to him. She put her hands on his chest and he cupped her breast, flicking a thumb over it. He kissed her deeply. She whimpered and moved her hand down to his engorged cock. He looked in her eyes. "Are you sure, sweetheart?" She nodded. He placed a finger between the folds of her cleft and rubbed her button. She was wet and ready. He lay on his back and pulled her on top of him. "When you're ready, sweetheart," he said.

She licked her lips and wiggled her hips until the head of his cock was at her entrance. She pressed into him, impaling herself, slowly. She lay on top of him and breathed deeply. She leaned on her elbows and kissed him. She took a deep breath and then began moving slowly. He moved his hands to her hips and moaned. "Yes, darling. Get it. Come for me. That's it. Get what you want." She picked up the pace and began to move faster, panting as she moved. She squeezed his cock between her cleft.

She moved quickly, as she felt the orgasm rippling

through her core, from deep inside her to her breasts and even to her head. She collapsed on top of him, breathing deeply. She moaned. "Alex. Alex." He held her hips tightly and pulled partially out of her and then in, firmly, the sound of her wetness creating a suction between them. Then she felt him quicken his pace. He thrust deeply, touching her womb. He enveloped her in his arms and thrust one more time before spilling himself inside her. He groaned, "Kara, yes, sweetness. Oh, yes." He rolled his head to the side and then back, capturing her lips in a sensuous kiss.

***

Alex had the medical specialist look in on Kara. As she was still rather nervous about being in the company of men she did not know, he remained in the room during Porter's examination. He took her blood pressure and listened to her heart. He examined her for swellings and broken bones. Since all seemed well, he gave her a bottle of pills and closed his bag. He looked at her and scratched his head. It appeared that she might be pregnant, but he didn't want to say so until he had a talk with her.

"Captain, can we have a minute of privacy?" Porter said, looking between the two.

"Is that OK with you, Kara?" Alex asked.

"Sure," she said, looking down at her hands. She'd been so tired lately; all she could do was sleep. She thought it might be the effect of the pirate attack. But perhaps the doctor was going to tell her differently. When Alex closed the door behind him, Porter turned back to her and smiled.

"Ms. Carlisle, I'm going to ask you some questions to clarify a diagnosis." She nodded and looked away from him.

"Can you remember when you had your last menses?" She frowned.

"Actually, I think." She paused, frowning. She had had a period, but it had been spotty. Her periods had often been irregular, so she didn't give it much thought. "I think it's been about a month ago, maybe six weeks. But I had it a little. Why?"

"Have you been feeling nauseous lately?" he asked. "Perhaps tender breasts." She gasped and hugged herself.

"What are you saying? What?" She sank back into the pillows.

"I'm asking you these questions because you may be pregnant." Silence. She looked at him as though she were looking through him. Her eyes were wide and her mouth pursed.

"I think you're wrong," she said. "I think this is just the effects of shock. I have been a little nauseous, but given the violence and the dead…" she stopped and looked around for the trash can. Realizing that she was about to vomit, he grabbed it for her and handed it to her. She threw up the breakfast she'd eaten, but thought it was just a matter of the upsetting emotions she'd felt after the pirate attack.

"I don't want to share this with Alex until I know for sure," she said. "I hope you can respect my privacy on this."

"Of course," he said. "It's just a theory. There could be other reasons for the symptoms you're having. Now," he put his hands on his thighs and rose. He was a tall man. Kara looked up at him. "Remember to take those pills I gave you."

"What are they?" she asked.

"Vitamins," he grinned. "Take care of yourself, Ms. Carlisle. I'll see you later." He left the room. Kara sat there, stunned. She placed a hand on her abdomen and looked down, smiling.

This was not something she wanted to hear, but when she gave it some thought, the news seemed to settle on her like a warm blanket. She might be having a baby. She remembered the first time she'd made love with Alex and considered whether it had happened then or later, after she'd come on board the Emma Ideal. Should she tell Alex? No, he would press her even more to marry. Marriage wasn't something she wanted right now. Maybe not ever. She thought back to the many vicious moments in her family life — the beatings, her mother also reacting weirdly to the circumstances, hiding herself away in her alcoholism.

She couldn't do that to a child. If she was indeed pregnant, she would have her baby, but she would be the only parent the baby had. She had enough money to start her own business as an accountant. She could set her own working hours from home. She thought about her apartment in New York. She'd already given it up. But she had a line on a place to live in Maine. This would work, but only if she could keep the news from Alex.

***

It took four more days to reach Cape Town. As the ship docked, Alex gave some of the crew a little time to go ashore while repairs were made. Some containers were offloaded while Harold Crane, the welder and fitter, and his coworker, Teo Saxton, made repairs to the ship. The pirates had tried to disable the ship without making it impossible to get to shore. However, they were not able to do as much damage as they'd hoped. Alex took a deep breath as he looked over the repairs.

He'd checked with his chief engineer and gave instructions to the second mate for the new course. He was making his way to his cabin when he saw a woman on shore trying to hail a taxi. The woman looked curiously like Kara. When she turned to look back at the ship, he could see that it must be her. He walked swiftly to his quarters and flung open the door. Her luggage was gone. He walked back to the ship's deck and descended the walkway.

He reached her in four quick steps. "Kara, sweetheart. Where are you going?"

She turned to face him. "I'm leaving, Alex. I don't think I can continue the trip."

"This is no way to leave, Kara," he said. "Weren't you even going to let me know?"

"I left you a note."

"A note!" he shouted. She jumped. He realized that his voice was carrying. The port was busy with vehicles moving quickly from here to there.

"Kara, let's go back to my cabin so we can talk about this. I'll help you get wherever you want to go, but please, let's don't do this here, out in the open for everyone to see." She looked up to the ship. A few of the crewmembers had gathered at the railings and were looking down. "I suppose you're right. It's just that you're so busy. I thought it would be better this way."

"No, let's go on board." He picked up her bag and escorted her back on the ship. When they got to his cabin, he sat down at his desk chair and she on his bed. She stood up again as though the bed scorched her behind, but realized from the smirk on his face that she was overreacting.

"Now, can you tell me why you've decided to leave without telling me about your plans?"

"I just think it would be better for me to go back to the states from here. I can catch a flight from Cape Town to New York; I've already booked a flight." He sighed and ran a hand down his face.

"Kara," he moved the chair to her and sat down in front of her. He picked up her hand and held it for a moment. "Do you remember that I asked you to marry me?"

"Yes, I remember," she said. She wasn't smiling — not a good sign.

"You never gave me an answer."

"I have the 'think-about-it' ring," she said, holding it up so he could see that she had not removed it from her ring finger. Her lips twisted slightly as though she were trying a half-hearted smile.

"What does that mean, Kara?" he looked down so that he could see her beautiful green eyes. He pushed a lock of her hair back from her face.

"It means I'm still thinking about it," she said. He stood suddenly and knocked over the chair. She flinched. He picked up the chair and stood it on its legs. He paced. Her eyes followed him about the room. He came to her and knelt in front of her on one knee.

"Sweetheart, maybe I haven't been clear enough about how I feel about you. I love you. Do you feel the same way about me?"

"I…Yes, I think. Yes I do," she said, trembling.

"Kara, either you do or you don't."

"I do, Alex, but I'm not ready for a commitment like marriage. It's just. I didn't have a good family life like you did. I don't want to make that kind of promise to someone."

"Is this about the pirate attack?" he asked. "Because if it is, you can't let that prevent you from living your life." She squeezed her eyes shut. It was like him to forget that she had a life before that attack.

"Yes, Alex. This is partly about the attack on the ship. It is about me killing another human being. It is about the violence. The bloodshed. The. Arguh." She stood up. The sudden movement made her dizzy; she sat back down on the bed with a plop. Alex frowned at her.

"Kara, are you alright? I mean. Are you sick or something? Are you? Is something wrong?"

"No, nothing's wrong. I just need to get off this ship. I can't go any further. I just can't." Tears began to slide down her cheeks. She began to sob. He gathered her in a hug.

"I understand, sweetheart," he said, kissing her forehead. "A cargo ship isn't a cruise ship. Things happen. My focus is getting the containers on this ship to their destination. That's what they pay me for, and I'm good at it." He kissed her lips and held her again. "I haven't had the time for you that I wanted to have. But I will. This is the last major run I'm making. I'm quitting after this. Future jobs will mostly be on land or not far from the shore. I was hoping that you would want to spend your life with me when I get to that place in my life, which will be very soon."

She looked up at him and sighed. "I just can't make a commitment like that. Not now. I'm not ready, Alex." She took the ring off and handed it to him.

"Here, you'd better take this. I don't want to make you think I can really make a commitment when I can't." He stood back with the ring in his hand.

"Kara, I want you to keep it." He slid it back on her finger. "I want you to have it as a gift from me. Whether you decide to be with me or not, I want you to have it as a reminder of our time together." He handed her tissues, and she blew her nose. She smiled as she thought it wasn't a very ladylike thing to do. He walked to his bathroom and wet a cloth to help her wipe her face.

"Let me at least help you get to the airport," he said. She nodded. "I have a few things I've got to do to make sure things run smoothly and then I'll be right with you. I'll have one of the crew get a cab for us." He left her in the room to tidy herself and went to the bridge. After a few arrangements, he was ready for the 20-minute ride to the Cape Town International Airport. Since it was late, there wouldn't be much traffic. The cab waited below.

He gathered her bags and escorted her there. The cab driver helped him store her luggage in the trunk. He got in and gave the driver the destination. He held her hand the entire way. When they arrived at the airport, he asked her which airlines she was planned to travel. South African Airlines stopped in Johannesburg but would get her back to the states in about 19 hours. He asked the cabbie to wait for him and escorted her to the porter.

He gave her one last hug and kiss and held her away

from him to look in her eyes. "You will stay in touch with me, Kara, right?" She nodded. "Yes," she croaked, her throat tight with tears. "I will. You have my contact info."

"Are you going back to New York or to Maine?"

"Probably somewhere near Portland, Maine. I...I." She sobbed. Tears rolled down her cheeks. She pulled out a tissue and wiped her face. He hugged her. "I'm sorry. I don't know what's wrong with me. I want to leave, but, but."

"It's OK, Kara," he said. "You don't have to explain. Just let me know when you land so I know you got there safely. As soon as I'm finished with this shipment, I'll be on a flight back to the states." He noticed some travelers trying to get around them and pulled her to the side. He took her face in his hands and peered in her eyes. He kissed her lightly on the lips. She felt a tingling on her lips and in her nether parts. She smiled.

"Kara, I love you. I think you love me too." She couldn't say it but she nodded and wiped her nose again. "I realize you can't make a commitment right now. But promise me you won't forget that I love you." She nodded again, this time vigorously. He smiled and hugged her again. "I'll see you when I get stateside again."

"Yes," she sobbed and took a deep breath. "I'm usually not this emotional. Sorry, Alex."

He hugged her again and picked up her bags. He checked them at the airline counter and took her as far as he was permitted to go.

***

Alex handed out the last of the pay as they docked in Singapore. When the eagle flew for the crew on his ship, everyone was ready for his or her share of the bounty. He said his goodbyes to the crew and lingered a while with the officers. He was in the bar having a drink when he noticed

Max and Porter sharing one too. He waved them over.

"What do you two plan to do now that we've delivered this shipment?" he asked. They sat together and nudged shoulders. It was no secret by now that they had a thing for each other. Alex figured as long as they didn't let it get in the way of their work, it was none of his business.

"We're going to sign on for another shipment," Max said. "We'll probably go with the same charter service. We'll decide when we get back to the states. There's a shipment going out of California. We're probably going to check that out." Porter winked at her.

"Speak for yourself. I might want to take some time off," Porter said. He tipped his glass up, emptying the whiskey into his mouth.

"I can't afford to take time off. I'm trying for a spot as captain," she said.

"I'm sure you'll make it," Alex said, smiling. "You've got what it takes."

"Hey, Cap," Porter said. "How's Kara? You heard from her yet?" He had an expectant look on his face. Alex frowned. He didn't think Porter had flirted with Kara, but you never know. He was known as quite the ladies man.

"Um, I've sent her a few email messages but just received a note that she arrived in the states, but nothing since then. Why? Are you planning to visit with her?"

"No, man. No," he smirked and looked at Max as though they shared a secret.

"OK, what's up? You two have a secret that you're not telling me," Alex said. "What is it? You two getting married or something? Max, have you heard from Kara?"

"As a matter of fact I have," Max said, wiggling her hips and puffing out her chest as though she was important. Alex was shocked. "You have?" his voice croaked or squeaked or something. He couldn't tell.

"So the two of you have kept in touch. How do you rate that, Max?" She shrugged.

"I don't know. We just…I had her email from when she reserved her passage and sent her a note asking how she was. She wrote back saying she's fine." She tried too hard to look nonchalant. Alex knew for certain that something was up. He'd played poker with both Max and Porter and knew neither of them were able to keep a straight face.

He toyed with his glass and looked in it as if there were answers there. Then he looked at both of them, first giving Max a careful look and then Porter. Both squirmed in their chairs.

"Alex, you might want to write to her again," Max said.

"I have written to her, but she doesn't answer me," he said, sighing. "Are you two going to tell me what's up or am I going to have to…to" he paused. There was nothing he could do.

"Look, Alex," Porter said. "I can call you 'Alex' now that you're finished with all this, right?" Alex nodded.

"If I were you, I would think about how she was feeling when she left and what that means. That's all I can say." Alex frowned.

"You think she's with someone else?" he asked. Porter blew out air and looked up to the ceiling. He looked at Alex and smiled.

"In a manner of speaking, could be," he said. "I can't say anymore. Just find her." That was all Alex needed. He pushed off the chair and put on his hat.

"It's time for me to leave; I have a plane to catch." He shook hands with both of them and picked up his bag. "Been a pleasure. You two be good."

CHAPTER TEN

When Alex arrived in Portland, not much had changed. He took a cab to his house in Buxton and unpacked. On the way to the states, he had pondered what Porter had told him. He had sent Kara several email notes but she had not responded. She did send a text saying that she landed safely in New York. That was a relief. But after that, he heard nothing from her. He wondered why. He'd tried texting her, calling her cell phone, but there was no answer. It wouldn't be the first time a woman had turned him down. He grimaced as he thought of it.

There was that time when Julie had decided that he wasn't what she wanted. They'd dated for a couple of years; but when Julie decided that her biological clock was ticking, she'd let him know that there was no future for them. She wanted a home and a family, but he was always out to sea.

Julie wasn't having it. She let him know that it was over. He was disappointed, but he saw it coming. This was the first time in about six years that he'd pursued a woman, really sought her and tried to win her. Sure, there had been a few brief encounters with women in between, but nothing serious. But he was wondering whether he would be able to get through to Kara, make a difference. He was hanging up clothes in his closet when an image of Kara flashed in his mind. Her soft skin, her throaty moans, her hot…Mmm. Maybe he shouldn't think about her. He could feel his cock getting hard as he thought about sliding into her sweet depths. He stood at the door of the closet for a moment, leaning his head on the door jam. If this went on for much longer, he'd have to take himself in hand, literally. Just then the phone rang. He walked to the dresser and picked up his cell.

"Hey, Mom," he said. "Yeah, I just got in."

"Hi, Alex," his mother said. "Everyone is here — your sister and her husband and your father. Can you come for dinner?"

"OK, yeah. I'll be there in a few hours. I have some things I've got to take care of in Portland, then I'll see you later today." His folks lived in Buxton too. Not far from his home. But they believed in visiting for days instead of hours. He didn't feel in the mood. He held his phone for a minute. He'd give Kara one more call before he went out. The phone rang but no one answered. "Damn!" He slammed the phone down.

***

Kara stayed in a hotel in Portland for a few days before she could find a townhouse for rent. She paid the hefty deposit and though the townhouse appeared to be clean, she always did her own extra preparations. She had the place cleaned to be certain it was ready. She returned to New York and had movers help her pack her belongings. In the process of moving things about, she'd put her cell phone down and couldn't find it. To make matters worse, she had had her computer packed as well. She shrugged. She told herself that it wasn't likely Alex was concerned about her. She had been in a fog since she returned. She was moving, but she wasn't sure this was the right thing to do. When everything was packed up, she stretched out on the bed to rest, but had fitful dreams instead. All she could feel was Alex poised to press his engorged member deep inside. She could feel the wetness between her thighs as she remembered his thrusts.

The next morning, she took a train from Penn Station to Portland. The six-hour ride gave her time to think. Killing a man was a difficult idea for her to cope with. She stared out the window and the rolling hills and winter landscape. Many of the trees were bare. She could see her reflection in the window. She licked her lips. She barely recognized herself. The bucolic scene seemed to fade from view as she saw the dead man before her, his eyes wide as he realized she'd shot him. Then, she saw the man who'd tried to take her off the ship. While she knew that it would have meant being kidnapped or raped or even killed, it was still difficult for her to come to terms with the idea that two men had been killed in her defense.

She thought back to those moments when the fight began. She closed her eyes tight, wishing the sounds and images would go away. The sounds of gunfire reminded her so much of the violence she'd experience as a child. The loud slap of the belt against flesh, the flinching and pain. She felt beads of sweat form on her brow as she thought back to the many times she'd been beaten by her stepfather — the times she could barely walk after the beatings — the times she'd lost consciousness. If she'd had a gun then, might she have killed her stepfather? She shivered at the thought.

She thought about the many times she'd considered running away from home to escape the beatings, but then had reconsidered. Life was hard out on the street. There had at least been plenty of food at home and with the exception of the beatings, she'd been able to cope with the crazy family life she had. She remembered times when her mother had been kind to her, buying her clothes and shoes, the times when they'd gone to a nice restaurant together, or times her mother visited her school performances. Could she forgive herself for killing another human being? If she had killed a human being, did that make her no better than her stepfather? Was it right to feel uncertain of Alex because he killed easily?

Her stomach twisted in knots as she considered these ideas. The experience of surviving such an event was more than she felt she could handle. How did Alex feel about this? He had killed a man in her defense. Did he regret it? Did he feel that it was wrong to take another human being's life, even if it was in self-defense?

How could she trust a man who killed so easily? Would he resort to violence in their personal lives? Could she trust him not to hurt her physically? The images of the man who tried to take her off the ship came to mind again. Her struggle with the pirate. The sound of the shot. The man's face was turned away from her, so she didn't see him, but she could see his body. She remembered not waiting to find out who had shot him. Undoubtedly, it was Alex. She'd crawled away so fast, so desperate to escape the chaos. She closed her eyes tight, trying to make the images go away. She took a drink of water and tried to forget — to doze on the train — but all she could feel was angry and irritable.

***

When her things were delivered in Maine, she went about unpacking some of the essentials she'd need to function, but still couldn't find her computer or cell phone. By now, both had lost power and would need a charge. She looked at all the boxes. The movers had been careful not to damage her clocks. She'd seen to those first. She decided to look for a grocery store so that she could stock the refrigerator. Fortunately, her place was within walking distance of every convenience she needed. She set out for Whole Foods and considered whether she might see Alex.

***

Alex walked into the door of his parent's home and smelled the home cooking. He had a key, as did his sister and brother-in-law. He took a deep breath and hung up his coat. It was early fall, but cold days began early in Maine. He walked into the kitchen. Everyone was gathered around the kitchen island. When they looked up and saw him, they sprung up from their chairs and mobbed him with hugs.

"Alex! You made it," his sister said. "Did you bring anyone with you?" She peered around him.

"No, I didn't, scamp," he said, giving her a hug.

"Hey, Ady, don't crowd the man. Give everyone else a chance to say hello." He gave his father a hug. Then his brother-in-law, Andrew gave him a manly half hug and pat on the back.

"So, how long are you here for, man?" Andy asked.

"I'm here for good."

"Eeeeee. Yes!" his sister began to jump up and down. "I knew you would do it. Do you really mean it, Alex? You're really going to stay home from now on?" He could see his mother's eyes tearing. He walked to her and hugged her.

"Hey. Now." Her lip trembled.

"I'm just so happy you're home, Alex," his mother said. "I'm even happier that you've decided to stop the cargo business."

"Mom, I told you my time was limited at that. Dad and I had talked about it some time ago."

"Right, but you didn't say when you'd be ready to make the change, son," he said.

"The change has come. I'm here to stay."

"Do you have some business prospects?"

"Yep. Have some lined up for the shipping business in Portland. I made those plans years ago. I'll be helping with a new effort to renew the cargo shipping business out of Portland."

"That's good news, son," his father said. "While you're at it, you can help me with the family business too."

"Hold up, wait a minute. Let's not move too fast. I have things to do here. We can talk about it. Meanwhile, I'm sure Andrew here is doing fine at helping you out."

"You're right about that," his father said, beaming at Andy. "However, whenever you're ready to pitch in, we'd be happy to have his lordship's help." His father smirked.

"Point taken, Da," he said. "Something smells good." He walked over to the range where his father was sautéing some shrimp.

"Trust Alex to arrive just in time for dinner," his sister said, rolling her eyes. "We were just about to sit down to eat. I'll lay out another place setting."

Alex rubbed his hands together. He sat at the table with his family and had big portions of stir-fried shrimp, lobster, rice, broccoli, corn, and an assortment of other nicely seasoned food. His father was the real cook, but his mother was able to put together a nice array of food as well. His sister had never learned to reach his father's level of cooking mastery and neither had he. But he liked to try. When they all finished helping with the dishes and cleanup, they went to the back yard to talk and later had a game of touch football. When he tired, he and his mother sat on the deck together and watched the three play. His sister was moving rather gingerly.

"So when is she due?" Alex asked. The question gave him the chills as he thought about whether Kara was "due" as well. He swallowed and looked blankly at the back yard as he wondered whether Kara might be pregnant. They hadn't been using protection some of the times they'd made love. Could it be? Surely she would tell him. He thought about how sweet she was the first time they made love, how hesitant. He had encouraged her to trust him. Had she learned to trust him as well? Would she tell him if she were pregnant? He felt something squeeze his chest as he considered having a child with Kara. He knew he loved her. His mind whirled with all the possibilities of their future. Why hadn't she called?

"Ady has about four months left," his mother said. Her ear-piercing whistle got their attention; she let one go when she noticed her husband making his way to an imaginary goal. "Way to go, honey! Show the kids how it's done!" The noise brought Alex back to the conversation with his mother.

"So why didn't we hear from you more often this trip, Alex?" she asked.

"I met someone, Mom," he said looking down. "I wrote to you about her."

"Right, I remember; Kara is it?" She looked at him to see his reaction but knew already that something disturbed him. He looked at his hands. They were folded, his elbows resting on his knees.

"I knew the minute you walked in that something was bothering you. We were hoping to meet her. What happened?" she asked. He sighed and leaned back on the picnic table.

"She came with me on this trip." He looked up as though searching for answers and looked back down and then at his mother.

"Alex, what do you mean? People don't usually travel on that route. How did she? I mean. Did she know?"

"No, she got on as a passenger. You know the charter service won't turn anyone away who pays for passage. She was on the ship before I realized it. After I found her, I couldn't send her back. Anyway, we would have lost valuable time if I had."

"You didn't want to send her back because there's

something special between you?"

"Yeah, Mom, I asked her to marry me."

"Wow! That's rich. Are we going to have a wedding soon?"

"I don't think so. She said no."

"Hmmm. Obviously, the woman needs…"

"Mom! Don't go there, please." She paused and looked at him carefully.

"Alex. Oh, Sweetheart. I'm sorry. You're in a lot of pain over this. There must be more to it than I thought." He ran a hand through his hair and looked to the left of where they sat.

"She…Mom, she was there when we were attacked by pirates. I think she's still in shock or something. I've been calling her for days, texting, emailing. No answer. I'm worried out of my mind. I can't imagine why she hasn't returned my calls or texted or something."

"Do you know whether she made it back to the states?"

"Yes, I put her on a flight out of South Africa and she texted me that she'd arrived in New York, but after that I haven't heard from her."

His mother took a few minutes to consider this and then turned to him. "Alex, when you say she was on the ship when it was attacked, exactly what happened?" The corners of his mouth pulled down, and he wiped his face with his hand.

"She shot a man who was trying to attack her," he said. "And I shot a second one who tried to kidnap her."

"That is some very serious stuff, Alex," she said. She took a moment to allow the others to pass them on their way into the house. She gave her husband that look by shaking her head slightly and he guided the other two into the house.

"Come on," he said. "I think we have some interesting desert in the kitchen."

"That banana, caramel dish?" Adelaide asked. "You'll

have to come inside to see," her father teased. Andy put his arms around her shoulder and helped her inside the house. He looked back at his brother-in-law. He knew the look as he had dealt with it not too long ago himself.

"So, Alex," his mother said. "In the years that I worked with patients in my clinic, I know that when a person experiences a traumatic incident such as what you're describing it can be very difficult to overcome. Not everyone responds to post traumatic stress in the same way."

"Post traumatic stress?" he asked. "You mean, you think she's still suffering? I thought as much, but I can't tell for sure because I can't find her."

"You must know, Alex, that when a person has experienced such trauma, one of the symptoms is a sort of disconnectedness with those they know." She paused to allow him to absorb the idea.

"Many times, a person who has experienced something of that nature will need some help and time to recover. She might be putting space between the two of you intentionally or without understanding what she's doing. She might even unwittingly associate you with the violence." He sighed and hung his head.

"I thought she might at least let me know where she is. She said she planned to move to this area, but how can I help her if I don't know where she is?"

"Well, that's a good sign."

"What."

"She's somewhere nearby. I'd bet on it."

"Really, Mom? How? I mean why do you think so?"

"If she made plans to be with you before the incident occurred, that means she has some serious feelings for you. She may be working through some other issues. Do you know whether she's had any traumatic incidents occur in her past?"

He looked off into the distance and thought back to

Kara's sharing about her family life. His brows moved up as though he realized something important.

"Yes, she had a troubled family life. I should have thought about that."

"So, she's probably working through this in her own way. Give her some time. She will likely get in touch with you when she's ready. That she hasn't contacted you recently doesn't necessarily mean she hasn't stopped caring for you."

"Why is it you always make sense, Mom?" he asked, smiling at her.

CHAPTER ELEVEN

Kara tossed on the small bed in her townhouse. Boxes still littered the rooms. She'd not been able to unpack completely for the two weeks she'd been there. She had no energy. Each night when she tried to sleep, she had nightmares. She'd wake in a sweat. The nightmares were all jumbled up. Sometimes she was at home as a child; other times she was on the ship with Alex. The man she'd shot became grotesque as each encounter become more bizarre. Sometimes, the man's face became her stepfather's. As she shot him, her stepfather fell before her. She'd wake up in a panic. Had she really shot her stepfather? Was it a dream? Why did she dream that? She felt angry at herself for allowing the feelings of guilt and shame to overcome her.

She might have done something else besides shoot the man. No, then, if she hadn't, the man would have, might have, dragged her away. He had that look in his eyes as he licked his lips. Did he lick his lips? What a stupid thought. I guess I could have shot him in the leg instead of the chest, she thought. Why didn't I think of that? Why didn't I point at a nonvital area? I was scared out of my wits; that's why. She shook her head and thought of the man lying there in a pool of blood. The thought sent her running to the bathroom for the hundredth time. She'd lost weight in the days since the incident had occurred. Why hadn't Alex called?

Oh, that's right. I can't find my phone in all this mess. She looked about her and tried to open one more box. The box was taped so tightly shut that she couldn't manage to get it open. She'd washed the two pairs of jeans and four blouses she'd packed in her large bag and had worn those as she looked for her clothing. Finding her other clothes was as challenging as finding her computer and phone. She sighed and looked at the mess her life had become. Her clocks hadn't been wound in days. There was none of the comforting noise from her collection of clocks. Some of them were packed up as well. She jumped as she heard a ping from what must have been one of the clocks.

"You've got to get out of here for a while," she said to herself. "You're losing your mind." She showered and brushed her hair and teeth. That seemed like a monumental task. As soon as she was finished, she wanted to crawl back into the bed. That alone tired her so much she wanted to pull the covers over her head and sleep some more. But she knew it was important to get some food. Whole Foods wasn't far away. She could slip in and out early in the morning. She dragged the jeans from the end of the bed and put them on and then a white blouse and sweater.

Desire at Sea

CHAPTER TWELVE

Alex liked stocking his fridge with the best organic vegetables he could find. So when he finished his business at Merrill's Marine Terminal, he got in his Volt and drove into town on Highway 1. He thought about what his mother said regarding Kara's state of mind and most of his anger at her fizzled out. Still, it was annoying that she didn't respond to his calls. He wanted to check on her to see how she was feeling.

He parked in the Whole Foods lot and plugged his Volt into the charging station. He turned to walk into the store and saw a woman who looked like Kara. He stopped in his tracks and stared at her for a moment, in his attempt to come to grips with her presence. She was much thinner than she'd been on the ship. He wasn't certain it was her.

But then he observed her smooth gait. Even as someone who appeared to be ill, she moved gracefully. She always seemed to float when she walked. "Kara!" he shouted. She kept walking. She didn't seem to hear him. He walked swiftly toward her. "Kara!" She turned and looked at him as though she didn't recognize him. Then she smiled. His heart leapt. But he could see after the smile faded that she was seriously ill. There were dark circles under her eyes and her once beautiful hair wasn't its glistening reddish brown. She seemed as though her life was ebbing away. Panic kicked him in the gut.

She stood there unmoving as though she could not believe it was him. She reached a hand out to his arm; then she began to sway. Her heart pounded. Her eyes fluttered and rolled back. She fell like a rock, hitting her head on the pavement. "Kara! Kara! Sweetheart!" He scooped her up in his arms and walked to a nearby chair. People were beginning to notice and stopped to gape. Trained in basic first aid, Alex began to check her pulse and feel for fever. She was warm, but not overly so. There was a knot the size of an egg near her temple. Her lips were pale as though she were dehydrated. He realized in an instant that she needed to be seen by a doctor.

He picked her up and carried her to his car. He bent to grab the door handle and pushed its button. The door opened; he bent down to place her gingerly in the car.

When he arrived at Mercy Hospital, hospital clerks and nurses checked her in immediately and assigned a doctor. They ran tests and administered an IV for fluids. She was still unconscious when they rolled her into a private room. He waited in the hall for a while as a couple of doctors checked her out. Then they allowed him in the room with her. Dr. Celena Flaherty came in to check Kara's vitals. She turned to him. "Are you Mr. Carlisle?" she asked.

"No, but I am her…" He paused. If they thought the two of them were not married, it was possible that they would not allow him to determine her care or to release her to his care if things should come to it. "I'm her husband. We share different last names." She nodded.

"Shall we go into the corridor Mr.…." she considered him with a questioning look. "It's Murdoch," he said.

"Ah," she said. "The Murdochs of Buxton. Alena and Jerry Murdoch? Your mother is a well respected psychiatrist."

Shit, she knew his family. "Yes, that's my family, my mom," he said. She stuck out her hand to shake his.

"I didn't realize you'd married Mr. Murdoch; it's Alex right?" she asked.

"Right. Can you tell me what the problem is with her? Is she going to get better? What happened? Why is she so thin and why did she faint? Why hasn't she woken up yet?"

Dr. Flaherty held up a hand and placed her stethoscope in a pocket of her white overcoat. "One at a time. I understand your anxiety here. She is quite dehydrated. She is a bit undernourished as well. I've examined her thoroughly. It seems she is suffering from some sort of mild case of the flu or some kind of virus possibly. But, her body has mostly fought that off…." she paused to allow him to digest the information. He looked to the floor and then up to her face. "Has she experienced some sort of trauma lately?" she asked.

"Um. Yes. But that was weeks ago."

"Weeks ago to you may seem a long time, but to someone who has experienced a trauma, it may seem like yesterday. I noticed quite a bit of movement of her eyelids, which suggests she might be dreaming of something traumatic. She also has murmured words that seem to suggest she was involved in a shooting of some sort. I didn't find evidence of an injury associated with it."

"She fell to the ground before I could catch her."

"I did find the knot on her head; that probably accounts for her having not regained consciousness. It's likely then she has a mild concussion. However, it's also possible that she is having a difficult time with whatever she experienced some time ago. Does she have a family physician?"

"No, she's new to the area. However, when she comes to, I'll ask her if she would like to use our family physician."

"That's a good idea. If she wants a different doctor, I would recommend you give her this list." She handed him a brochure. "There are other doctors she might consider. Included in that list are some doctors who specialize in psychiatric cases such as the one she might have. I'm not a specialist in this area, but the general assessment is that she might be suffering from post traumatic stress disorder."

"I've been told that's possible." She nodded as though she thought it only natural that his mother might have given him some hint of what Kara was suffering.

"Why didn't you bring her in before now?" Well, that was a good question, he thought. He didn't want to tell the doctor that he didn't know where she was, so he adjusted the truth a bit.

"I've been out of town for a while. I realized she was sick when I saw her for the first time today." The doctor nodded her head as though considering the veracity of his claim.

"At any rate, I would recommend you take her home and stay nearby. She shouldn't be alone under the circumstances. Watch her carefully. Get her away from anything that might remind her of the incident. Long walks in nature are good. Try to get her to talk about it."

"Are there any other symptoms I should watch for doctor?" he asked.

"You might notice that she tries to avoid activities, she could have some flashbacks, some rapid heartbeats and breathing, nausea, sweating. Much of this mimics flu-like symptoms, so don't confuse those two."

"You said she had some sort of virus or the flu," he said.

"This might have been a result of the initial symptoms that may have compromised her immune system. Extreme stress can do that. The stress makes it possible for opportunistic infections to develop. But, as I said, that's really not an issue for her at this time. The important thing is to get her rehydrated and strong again."

"That's no problem."

"I'm asking that you keep her here overnight. She's likely to wake in the night. If that happens, reassure her that she is here and safe." He nodded.

"And, Alex, Mr. Murdoch, be sure to take care of yourself. Overcoming this kind of trauma can be hard on family members. We have treatment programs for it. However, the best cure is the love and support of family. Some people recover quickly while others take some time to recover. So be careful that you find a balance for yourself."

Alex nodded. He sat down in a chair across from Kara after the doctor had left the room. He thought for a while about his sister. Funny thing to think about at a time like this, but he supposed it made sense in a way. Ady had been ill years ago. His mother had recognized her symptoms immediately and put her in therapy. He remembered feeling helpless then. He felt helpless now. Did he want to go down this road again? Could he help Kara when he couldn't do a damn thing to help his own sister? He stood up and walked to her bed and held her hand. She didn't seem to know he was there. But she sighed. That was a good sign.

CHAPTER THIRTEEN

Kara woke to the sounds of birds outside. It was cold in the room. She looked around. The room didn't look familiar. It wasn't the hospital. She'd woken up briefly there. She remembered things in a haze of blurred images, Alex hugging her, saying they were leaving the hospital and then falling asleep again in his car. She yawned. She vaguely recalled him bringing her to this room and tucking her in bed.

"Hey, sleepy head," he said grinning. His muscled chest was bare. He wore just his skivvies, which hugged his tight glutes. He was eye candy. "You're finally up."

"Alex!" She reached for him. He came to the bed and enveloped her in a hug. He kissed her tenderly, but then with hunger. He pulled back, panting.

"You had us all worried for a while, Kara," he said. "How are you feeling?" She pulled back from him and felt the lump on her head.

"Like I've got a headache and a knot on my head to prove it." She laughed softly. "Where am I?"

"You don't remember me bringing you here?"

"Mmm. Vaguely, yes. I think. I'm not sure."

"I brought you here because someone needs to watch you and I don't know where you live," he said, smirking. "We need to talk about that and some other things, but first…."

"First, I need to get a bath or shower or something and get changed," she said. "Where are my clothes?"

"They cut them off you. You'll have to wear one of my shirts. That should be long enough to cover you until I can get your clothes. My sister left a pair of jeans and some other stuff here sometime back. You two look about the same size. That should do until we can get your own. My housekeeper washed some new underclothes my sister bought for you. I hope you don't mind."

"No, of course not. Is your sister here?"

"She went back to my parents' place. She and her husband are visiting for a bit. If you feel up to it later, we can go by there." She yawned.

"Where's your bathroom?" He swept a hand behind him.

"Your majesty's bath awaits her." He smiled and scooped her up.

"Hey! I can walk on my own!"

"I know, I just wanted to be sure you get there without incident. Plus," he said, kissing her on the nose, "It's been a long time since I've seen you naked."

She relaxed and put her arms around his neck. He walked into the bathroom, which was covered in marble-like tile. Its spacious interior included a large, heated, whirlpool tub that was already filled and waiting. Nearby was glass-enclosed shower that appeared to have a steamer.

"Mmm. You seem to come prepared to have fun in your bathroom," she said.

"It was this way when I bought it," he said smiling. "However, if it weren't I'd have put in similar accommodations. He stood before the tub with her in his arms.

"You are going to put me down aren't you?" she said, smiling. "I wouldn't want you to fall as you're getting into the tub with me in your arms. That wouldn't be very romantic." She giggled. Good sign, he thought. She's getting back to the Kara I know.

"It just so happens that I'm an expert at getting women to bathe, madam," he said.

"You are?" she asked.

"I am."

"And who else have you done this for?" While they talked he had stepped into the tub and lowered them both. She didn't realize it until she felt the water envelop her. It was warm and smelled of lavender and eucalyptus.

"No one but you, sweetheart. I do have my ways at encouraging the women in my family with bath oils and such." He reached under the water and took off his shorts. He balled them up and threw them in the sink next to the tub. The wet cloth created little sprinkles of water. She closed her eyes and opened them to see him looking intently at her.

"You do! Well. I think I'd like to see some of those encouraging products too."

"You're getting the first introduction to one now," he said, smiling. The tub was big enough for two to sit in. He reached to the edge and picked up some cloths and soap. "I'm going to help you clean up."

He washed her face gently and then rinsed it, being careful of her eyes. Then, he laved the cloth again with a large bar of lavender soap. He washed her neck and arms, then slowly washed each breast and her stomach. She could feel fluttering in her abdomen. He rinsed her. As he turned to get more soap, she could see his erection poking up out of the water. She put her hand on it and rubbed its head. He closed his eyes. "If you keep doing that, I'm not going to be able to finish your bath, princess."

She grinned and kissed him lightly on the lips. "Mmm."

The sound of his pleasure rumbled through his chest. She could feel it vibrating through her. He placed the washcloth between her legs and began to rub her lightly there. She relaxed even more against the back of the tub. The designers of the tub made it difficult for a person to slide fully into the water with indentations and grips in the tub. He rinsed her and then paid the same careful attention to both her legs and then her feet, where he massaged each toe on her foot. She dunked her head under the water to wash her hair.

"Alex," she said. "You're making me forget all about food."

"We're going to get to that soon," he said smiling. He gave himself a quick wash too. The water jets massaged her aching back muscles. "This is a wonder tub, Alex. If I took a bath in this thing every day, I might not get out for several hours."

"That's why I rarely use it when I'm home," he said. "I usually use the shower. But I thought you'd enjoy the heated water and massaging jets." She frowned. Was he planning on going back out to sea soon?

"You're right. It's heavenly." He stood and stepped out of the tub. He reached for two plump white towels. He dried himself and wrapped the towel around him, then turned to lift her from the tub. He set her on the bath mat and began to dry her too. He grabbed another towel, which he gave her to dry her hair.

When they entered his bedroom, she walked to the bed and sat on it. He walked to her and lifted her face to his. He bent and kissed her. "Kara, you don't know how much I've missed you. You almost broke my heart when I didn't hear from you."

"I lost my cell phone," she said, tears began to well in her eyes. "I haven't been myself lately. I don't know what's wrong. I'm usually very neat and organized. But when I moved my stuff from New York here, I misplaced it and my computer. For some reason, I haven't had the energy to find either of them. I've just...."

"Shhh. It's OK, sweetheart. You've been under a lot of strain lately."

"What do you know about it? You weren't here. My apartment is full of boxes! I can't find anything and I don't know that I want to." He sat down on the bed beside her.

"Kara, I'll help you with that, but first," he kissed her. She could feel the space between her legs getting moist. He flicked his tongue over her bottom lip and placed a hand on her breast where he gave the same attention to one of her nipples. His hand drifted to her center where he began to rub her clit, back and forth. Then, he laid her back on the bed, spread her legs and found the nub with his tongue. She jumped and squirmed. "Alex! Please." He kissed her from her thighs to her neck and came over her to place the tip of his erect penis at her entrance.

He kissed her again and slid into her wet heat. He rested there a moment to allow her time to get accustomed to his girth. Then he began to move, slowly at first, then faster. He pulled out and pushed back in making her think he would withdraw completely and then surged back into her. She felt herself nearing orgasm and then it came; she exploded, wave after wave of delicious spasms that radiated from deep within her and made her feel warm and loved. As she neared the end of the contractions, she felt Alex surge into her, once, twice, then utter a series of nonsensical words as he spewed his juice deep inside her.

His weight felt good on top of her, but he rolled off her soon. She had lost so much weight; he didn't want to hurt her. They dozed for a few minutes as he gathered her close. When they woke, they washed again and went to the kitchen.

He had a feast prepared for her. There were pineapples, bananas, oranges, grapes, an assortment of breads, an apple walnut salad, and the makings for eggs benedict. He prepared one for both of them, resting the poached egg on top of a crab cake and spreading it with rich hollandaise sauce. She licked her lips as her mouth watered. He set the plate before her, and they relished their meal at the kitchen counter.

"Alex, this is so delicious; how did you learn to make this?"

"My father is the cook in our family, but we all take turns trying to outdo one another. It's like a hobby for us."

"It's a wonder you're not much heavier than you are if cooking is a family occupation."

"I said we like to cook. I didn't say we liked to sit around doing nothing but cook," he said smirking. When they finished the meal and had tea and coffee, he placed the dishes in the dishwasher and returned to the counter to sit with Kara.

"Kara, we really didn't finish talking about your situation," he said.

"I'm sorry I didn't make more of an effort to reach you, Alex. I've been a mess lately. I moved here without thinking it out. I guess I should have stayed in New York. I think." She paused. She got out of the chair and walked to the doors that led to his deck. Her back was to him as she looked out into his back yard. There was nothing but land there. The day was grey and overcast as though it might snow any moment. She turned to face him.

"I wanted to be near you even though I wasn't sure how I felt exactly," she said.

"And now?" he asked.

"I love you, Alex," she said turning to him. "But I feel guilty for shooting that man. I can't seem to stop thinking about it. I guess a part of me feels like I don't deserve the love I feel for you. There's not a day that goes by that I don't think about taking a person's life. I *took* a life." He left the chair and walked to her. He put his arms around her and drew her tightly to him.

"Kara, I'm so happy to hear that you love me because I love you too." He paused and kissed her deeply. He came up for air and looked in her eyes. "But, the guilt you feel is something that many people experience when they've experienced trauma. The doctors say that you might be experiencing post-traumatic stress disorder."

"PTSD?" she looked puzzled. "I've heard about that. I thought it only happens to soldiers who go to war."

"It can happen to anybody who has experienced something traumatic. It doesn't have to be a death." He paused a moment and looked down into her face hoping she would put together her earlier trauma as well as part of her symptoms.

"Ahh!" she said. "You mean that what happened to me as a child could also be complicating matters." He breathed, relieved that she had put it together.

"Smart girl," he said. "Usually, it takes a little therapy for people to overcome it. The worst thing you can do is cut yourself off from your support system, people who love you."

She walked back to the counter and sat in her chair. She fingered the napkin that had been part of her place setting. She wore the "think-about-it-ring" that Alex had given her. She looked at it and twisted it about. Alex inhaled, hoping she wasn't about to try to return it again.

"I think I don't need this ring anymore, Alex," she said. His stomach knotted. "It's funny how I lost everything else but not this ring."

She looked up at him. "I think I'm finished thinking about it. If the offer is still good, I want to…I want us to be engaged if you still want to. I mean." Alex felt the knot unfurling in his stomach. He walked to her and lifted her from the chair. He hugged her to him.

"Oh, Kara, sweetheart. You've made me so happy."

CHAPTER FOURTEEN

A few days later, when Kara was feeling better, she took Alex to her townhouse where he helped her take boxes of her things to their new home, the home where Alex had lived by himself when he was in town for short periods, but that he would now share with Kara. Adelaide and Andy welcomed Kara to the family and helped with the moving of boxes. After Alex explained things to her landlord, she was able to transfer her lease to a friend of Alex's. His parents loved her as well. They took long walks in the woods and spent many quiet hours together. Kara joined a group of people who also had suffered from some sort of trauma, and gradually she engaged in the healing process.

In the spring of the following year, Alex and Kara had a big wedding in Portland, where they enjoyed the company of her friends and his as well. When the excitement was over, they left for a honeymoon in Canada. She whispered to him on one of the many short rides they'd taken. She was expecting their first child. They shared many happy years together.

Desire at Sea

Desire at Sea is a work of fiction. Names, characters, places and incidents are products of the writer's imagination or have been used fictitiously and are not to be construed as real. Any resemblance to persons living or dead, actual events, places, incidents or organizations is coincidental.

Cover design by Tatiana Villa of Villa Design.

ABOUT THE AUTHOR

Ela Bell lives with her husband on an island in the Gulf of Mexico. She enjoys playing the piano, reading and traveling. She is a member of RWA, has a degree in literature and has written stories and poetry for many years. She enjoys hearing from readers. Write her at elabell19@gmail.com.

Read other stories by Ela Bell related to *Desire at Sea*.
The Hot Desire Series
Heat
Hot
Engaging Passion

Blog with Ela Bell at Narrativemagic.com.
http://www.narrative-magic.squarespace.com/ela-bell/

Review *Desire at Sea*.
Would you like to receive a newsletter from Narrativemagic.com about Ela Bell's upcoming novels? Write at narrativemagic@gmail.com